THE SPACE BETWEEN THE SEASONS

Justice Tilsher

Text copyright © 2023 Justice Tilsher.

Book cover by MiblArt

Interrior illustrations by Atik Sugiwara

www.justicetilsher.com

ISBN: 979-8-9875314-0-2

Download the *free* original song, *Whirlwind.*

justicetilsher.com/whirlwind

To my sister, Kyree,
for being the greatest friend I could ever ask for
— J.T.

1

Although their advancement in society had been far from an easy climb, the two grown-up Everleigh sisters had successfully laboured their way out of the workhouse years ago. They now rented a small home on the outskirts of town and enjoyed a steady income. Autumn particularly had put in a lot of work, sweat and determination to improve their station. They had earned their place in the world.

The fall months brewed just beneath the surface of the atmosphere, creeping up the bark of old trees and consuming the leaves with subtle fragrance. Their crisp, golden scents kissed the cooling air. England seethed with innovation and development, with Queen Victoria several years into her fourth decade on the throne.

"Patience! Get out of the way, will you?" Autumn entered the kitchen on shaky legs. Icy water from the large cast-iron pot in her arms spilled over its rolled edges and sloshed down her dress.

"Let me help you!" Patience answered brightly, not budging an inch.

"I've got it. Just look out!"

Patience moved to the side, frowning. Her sister trudged ahead, squeezing her eyes tight and trying to ignore the painful weight in her grasp. Her foot caught on a stray whisk and she skidded forward.

"Oh!"

"Careful, careful!" Patience caught the base of the pot. "Quick!"

Liquid flew over them both and gushed across the floor, flooding the cramped space.

"Go, go, go!" The sisters heaved the pot, clanging the base on the stove with such force that a good deal of the remaining water sprang free.

Patience shuddered, clutching her side as she bent over. Her face deepened in colour.

"Nasty water." Autumn puffed up her cheeks and wiped her dripping hands across her grimy apron. "Pay-pay, I told you I didn't need your help!"

Patience breathed heavily as she dipped her fingers in the pot, pulled her hand back and splashed her sister playfully.

"Oh!" Autumn's mouth dropped open in cold shock as her muscles tightened. She gave a long blink and laughed. Cupping water in her hands, she gave Patience a good splash in return.

"Hooray! The spell is broken. The witch's magic has released me!" Patience raised her hands high above her head and pirouetted across the room.

"And now the beautiful princess Patty may return home to her fair sister." Autumn bowed, smiling as she held out the left side of her stained dress. She flourished a spatula, doing her best to look regal.

"Stop it, I'm blushing." Patience put a hand across her chest and batted her eyelashes.

Autumn giggled, peering into the pot to see bubbles lightly forming below. "Now. Where are the vegetables?" She glanced around the kitchen.

"Under the table!" Her sister waved a floppy hand and threw a rag across the floor to sop up the water.

Autumn began to pile an assortment of greens onto the table in the centre of the room.

"I can't wait for everyone to arrive!" said Patience, getting down on her hands and knees and wringing out the wet cloth in a wooden bucket.

"Yes. You have said so before..." Autumn deftly minced an onion with a sharp knife. She must remember to thank Mr. Pickerly again for the vegetables. *And I mustn't forget the promise I made to him, to help him husk the last of his corn this week.*

Odd jobs around the Pickerly farm made a not insignificant contribution to their income and the sweet gentlemen often sought Autumn's assistance. Every penny earned was saved for a future home for herself and her younger sister. Autumn had been scrimping and saving for years, pitching in at the farm whenever she wasn't schooling the Glendale children at the Raven's Nest household.

All Autumn's hard work would soon pay off. She just needed a few more pounds for the down payment on her dream home. She closed her eyes and pictured the two-story building in her mind: it possessed a brick chimney and a tall pine tree out front. A creamy white trim decorated the doorframe. The ground floor would be home to the bakery: her bakery. Imagine, making pastries for a living and working for yourself, never again relying on the aid of an employer to decide your fate! And then, of course, there was the floor above; beautiful, spacious living quarters with room for both her and her sister to be quite comfortable. It was a world away from the tiny one-bedroom house they shared now.

"Off to dreamland?" Patience smirked, tapping her sister on the shoulder and breaking her reverie.

"Mm?" Autumn cocked her head, blinking. Her eyes drifted to the vegetable in her hand. "Oh, I am only thinking of the house. You know the one with the—"

"White doorframe. I know, I know." Patience rolled her eyes, as she set the pail of water to the side.

"Do I talk about it all that much?"

"Hardly ever," answered her sister, a touch of sarcasm in her voice.

Autumn picked up the cutting board and used the knife to guide the produce into the soup. "Do you suppose payment from Mrs. Glendale has arrived?"

"I can't see how you'd have missed it. You've been at the window every five minutes for the past few hours..." Patience brushed against her sister's shoulder and lifted her eyebrows up and down before taking up a knife.

"Patty, you put that down this instant. You could cut yourself!"

"But you use it all the time!"

"Because I am always careful."

"I'm careful too!"

"You? Careful? Just this morning you almost broke your neck attempting a cartwheel."

"I only bruised an arm."

"Exactly! Bruised arm today, broken neck tomorrow."

"Let me use the knife, please! Let me help."

"No."

"Autty. I am twenty years old, for goodness' sake."

"Oh, don't start that again," Autumn huffed. "Protecting you is my job, and you certainly don't make it easy! Reminding you to look out when you're in the street, preventing a—"

"Boring, boring." Patience touched her fingers together, moving them up and down on top of her thumb to mimic her sister's mouth moving as she spoke.

"Oh, Patience, please! Get started on the sponge cake, if you want to help me," Autumn giggled, shooing her sister with a dust cloth as Patience scurried over to search a cabinet.

Autumn dropped the last ingredients into the soup, causing a droplet of hot water to bounce onto her skin. She winced.

"Don't you loathe the dining room, Patience? Far too old-fashioned. And that awful-"

"You are inventing problems. Excuses to move."

"I am not!" Autumn blinked. The rays of sunlight coming in the window seemed to send the floating dust cascading down a river of bright light. "This place is wretched. And it isn't *ours*—" Her eyes refocused on her sibling. "No, no—use the large bowl." She shoved past her sister and rummaged around in the cupboard before producing the appropriate vessel. "See?" Autumn brandished the bowl, then slammed it on the table.

"Yes, yes." Patience grabbed the flour and measured several overflowing cups.

"How many cups is that?"

"Uhm... five?"

"You were only supposed to use three! Honestly! Just- just let me do it." She pushed her sister aside, taking the instrument from her hand. "Go and fetch some eggs, will you?"

Patience mumbled something under her breath that Autumn couldn't hear as she flounced from the kitchen.

Autumn added a teaspoon of salt and a dash of sugar to the mix.

"Autumn?" Patience set two eggs on the table, deftly stopping one from rolling off onto the floor just in time. "These are the last eggs. We shan't have any left for breakfast tomorrow!"

"Are you sure? I could have sworn we had plenty this morning."

"I- three of them were broken, remember?"

"Bother." Autumn reached for an egg and cracked the shell on the rim of the bowl. "I shall have to visit the market in the morning. I haven't the time to go all the way into Carlisle before supper today."

"I can go and get some now, if you like!" Patience said, clasping her hands together. Her eyes sparkled at the thought.

"Oh, no, you could not. If I wanted you to risk your life on the way to the market, I would have granted *that* request a long time ago."

"But I've been to the market dozens of times with you. I know the way like the back of my hand!" She thrust a hand in her sister's face as if to prove her point.

"And I know *you* like the back of *my* hand! You will run all the way there, falling and skinning your knees seven times over, all so you can hurry to stop by the bookshop!"

Patience's frown concealed a smile. "But I have read all my books more than ten times over! I am getting tired of reciting the chapters from memory..."

Autumn began mixing the batter. "We shall go to the bookshop within the coming week, then."

"I know I could go on my own. I promise I will be extra careful and never talk to strangers."

"You always say that and yet you have a nasty habit of asking anyone you meet for assistance. The world isn't all butterflies and sunshine. Meeting the wrong person just once could ruin your life, take away all—"

"What if I took a carriage instead?"

"A carriage? Have you lost your mind? You know how much I detest those contraptions! Didn't you hear of the accident outside the gentlemen's club on Fourth Street only last week? Why, with your luck you would certainly be next! And I would—"

"Autumn." Patience put a hand on her sister's shoulder, her face lit with her biggest smile. Autumn rolled her eyes, trying unsuccessfully not to laugh as she bent over the dough bowl, the ring on her necklace bouncing against her chest.

"Honestly, will you kindly find something else to do other than torment me with your deadly wishes?"

"I want to help you get ready for Mr. Williams arriving!" Patience drew back and crossed her arms.

Autumn glanced around the kitchen, sighing deeply. "Everything is in hand. Occupy yourself until dinner, somewhere other than the kitchen." She lifted a big spoonful of the batter before letting it slowly drip back into the bowl. Yes, just the perfect texture to make the finest sponge cake. She had almost perfected her recipe. The company tonight would be well fed indeed!

"Autumn, where is the morning paper?"

"I think I left it in the drawing room."

Patience left, leaving Autumn content with her baking while staring out the open window at the orange foliage scattered about the front yard, begging to be picked up by the cool breeze. The birds chirped as they prepared for the winter months. She closed her eyes and hummed a tune.

"Would you look at this!" Patience stormed back into the kitchen with full force, her wide eyes on the newspaper. "Construction has started on the Clarkson Memorial!" She used a free hand to tap blindly along the counter until she found the jar of biscuits. "Can you imagine how *glorious* it will be once completed!" She stuffed a biscuit into her mouth.

"Patience, you will ruin your appetite!" Autumn scolded. She smiled at her sister's enthusiasm. Patience shared her every thought with Autumn; to her older sister, she was an open book. Autumn, on the other hand, kept most of her thoughts hidden away within the pages of her journal, the only confidante she trusted.

"Listen to this!" Patience spoke through a full mouth as she flipped to the next page. "Must-visit travel destinations: Blackpool, Wales, and Yorkshire! I shall very much like to take my box-camera there one day and compare the landscapes to the ones here in Carlisle."

"I imagine they are about the same. You can't be missing much."

"Perhaps," she said, turning the page. Her mouth dropped open. "Look! Mr. Williams has an article on his return from the jungles of Africa! How jolly!"

"Jolly, indeed. I don't suppose he will appreciate all the hard work we are going through to give him this supper tonight."

"He will!" Patience nodded vigorously, a smile forming across her lips. "Can you believe it's been five months since he left for his travels? It feels like a lifetime ago!" She gave a little jump, hugging the newspaper against her chest with both arms. "Imagine the fun he must have had..." she closed her eyes, drawing in a long breath through her nose.

Autumn cocked her head. "Fun? For someone like him, maybe. That man is something else—a lunatic at best."

"Sister, you never were fond of him. Why must you resent him so?"

"The man has no common sense. Picture traveling around the world all the time and putting your life in the hands of ships and trains and being dependent on foreign tongues! I shall faint thinking of it!"

"It sounds exotic!"

"Hah. It sounds scandalous. I feel bad for the woman he marries."

"I shall think her lucky."

"Lucky? That man is no different from any other. Selfish, unreliable, and a born liar. Worse than that, even, putting his life on the line and spending money carelessly all the while."

"He never lied."

"He didn't lend you that book like he promised to, now, did he?"

"Autumn, he simply forgot! It happens to the best of us."

"Broke his word, more accurately, which happens to the worst of us and those of whom you should be most wary."

"But he is always so kind! Didn't you know that he helped his friend marry a woman once on one of his expeditions? How romantic..." Patience snatched a dry dishcloth and wrapped it around her head, giving a drawn-out blink.

"A fragile union that will break no doubt. You know what I always say, marriage is—?"

"A house of cards, yes, Autumn. I know."

"Precisely. One that might come crashing down at any moment."

Patience nodded, eyes drifting toward the window, hands still holding the cloth around her golden curls.

"Angola's African jungles..." she sighed, voice softening. "Now that is certainly a wonder in and of itself; you can't deny that now, can you?"

"In a heartbeat."

"I shall have so many questions for Williams upon arrival. Do you think he saw many snakes? He must have! I shall have to ask him if the gorillas are as large as the books claim them to be."

Autumn shook her hair from her face. "I am sure that he will be more than thrilled to tell you all about his nasty travels for hours upon hours tonight. And that is *Mister* Williams to you." She covered the dough and focused on the stack of plates on the countertop. How many were they entertaining tonight? She squinted, trying to remember.

"Sorry. *Mister Williams*," Patience dramatically corrected herself, tossing the newspaper aside.

"You consider yourself quite the lady, yet you can't remember proper courtesy." Autumn clicked her tongue in shame. "Three... four... five..."

she counted while touching each plate. Had she remembered everyone? Mr. and Mrs. Pickerly, Mr. Williams, and... "Patty, is it six people tonight, or five?"

"Five!"

Autumn removed a plate.

Patience took the wine glasses from the cupboard and set them on the countertop. "Oh! It is six!"

Autumn bit her lip and replaced the spare plate on the stack, eyes drifting to the window. "Oh! It's here! Patience don't touch the stove. The last thing I need is for you to get burned."

"I won't get burned."

Autumn bit her lip as she eyed her sister and the stove. "On second thought, don't touch anything while I am gone. I won't be but a minute!"

And away she went, out of the kitchen and to the front door. Stepping outside, she felt the vibrant afternoon sun soak into her skin. *Goodness, is fall always this beautiful?* Autumn closed the door behind her as she took in a deep breath of the fresh air.

Looking beyond the untrimmed shrubbery and the huge maple tree, Autumn could see the lake that bordered their small property. Closer to their muted brick home, with its decaying roof, were clothes hanging on the clothesline.

Autumn turned her attention from the scenery to the path as a servant from the Ravens Nest hurried over.

"Please, God," she whispered to herself and closed her eyes as she hoped, her heart creeping into her mouth.

"Greetings, miss!" The servant handed Autumn a slim envelope and went on his way.

Autumn thanked him and wasted no time in tearing open the envelope to reveal the lovely banknote.

"Oh!" She hugged her monthly payment against her chest with as much pressure as she could muster. "Patience!" Autumn hurried back inside. She quickly stepped across the threshold without bothering to close the door. One moment the air was filled with the scent of the crisp day outside, the next it was replaced with the warm scents of supper cooking.

"Patience!" Autumn burst into the kitchen like a whirlwind, waving her prize back and forth with frantic movements.

"What?"

"Oh, Patience!" Autumn danced around her sister in circles, stuffing the banknote into her apron pocket. She pulled the newspaper away from her sister and set it on the countertop, despite protests that Patience was yet to finish reading.

"Our life is finally going to change for the better!" She pulled her sister in close and squeezed her in a tight embrace. "I never thought this day would come," Autumn whispered, tears glazing her cheeks. "I prayed and prayed, but I also doubted. And now my hard work has finally paid off."

She broke the embrace and grasped Patience's hands in her own. "Just wait until you see this house. I have planned it all, everything! The big rug shall go in my room and the hall table in yours! And we will buy a window seat where you can lie and read your books! Patience, did I mention that the house has a special door connecting our bedrooms? We can lie in bed and talk, each in our very own room!" She lifted her pointer finger to wipe the joyful tears from her eyes.

Patience said nothing, just lifted one side of her mouth in a smile.

"And we shall buy new wallpaper and dress it with lilies, your favourite!" Autumn focused on their hands, seemingly composing herself, before she slowly raised her gaze to meet her sister's. "We will be so happy there." She sighed, more tears dripping free.

Patience forced a tight smile.

"Patty?" Autumn cocked her head, eyebrows furrowing. "Is something upsetting you? You snuck more biscuits, didn't you? I told you not to eat them before supper."

Patience shook her head, gaze falling to the floor. "I feel fine."

"Well, you don't look fine. Something must be wrong. Did you stay up late last night?"

Patience's face morphed into a warmer smile as she squeezed her sister's hand. "I am happy for you Autumn, that's all." Her voice cracked. "Honestly, I am. You will be very content in that new house."

Autumn could have sworn her sister was about to cry. "Patience, this isn't just for me. It's for us both. Think of the memories we will create together."

Patience sighed, letting her gaze drift to the kitchen window. "But what if there's something missing...?"

Autumn cocked her head, heartbeat rising. "Patty, you are scaring me. What are you saying?"

"This." She pulled away and cupped her hands. "The house you want to buy, the rooms you will fill, the door between the bedrooms, the new wallpaper... that is what you want and have wanted for many, many years, and believe me, I am happy for you. It's only..." Patience closed her mouth, her cheeks filling with colour.

Autumn reached forward and put her hand under her sister's chin. Patience made no eye contact. "Patience?"

"Have you ever stopped and asked yourself... what a life *outside* of Carlisle might be like?"

Autumn touched her teeth together and parted her lips. "No, I—"

"Well, I have!" Patience's words became more passionate as she dropped her hands to her side. "Autumn, our life has been the same every day for as long as I can remember! We wake up, go to work at the Raven's Nest, and go to bed. Each day my life is the same: you telling me what and what not to do. I cannot get dressed, go outside, or even speak without some word of caution coming from your self-proclaimed all-knowing mouth, and I am tired of it!"

Autumn gasped and put her hand over her heart.

"Autumn," Patience's voice pitched higher as she gestured to the window. "I have never, ever been outside of this town. Not even once! I have never seen London, I have never been to Yorkshire, or... or Wells! For all I know these are merely fictitious locations people use to fill the news and conversation with. Autumn, I want to *go* to these places! I want to go beyond them! I want to take off my shoes and run in the grass without any sense of judgment or word of warning! I want to use my camera and take pictures of the whole wide world!" She picked up the newspaper and held a page up to her sister's face. "Isn't this beautiful?"

Autumn blinked a few times, stepping back to get a better look at the flowers in the picture. "A meadow?"

Patience pulled the paper away before her sister could process the image any further. "It's not about meadows, Autumn; it is about freedom! Imagine seeing the rest of England, comparing the shores and meeting the different people! Imagine seeing more of Europe or traveling to North America, China... beyond!"

Autumn's lower lip trembled, coinciding with her shaky arms. "I- I don't quite know what to say."

"Nothing," Patience set the article aside and touched her sister's cheek, her hand cold. "Say nothing. I spoke with Hortense at her ball last week, and she invited me to go with her to France this coming January. She asked me to bring the camera Mr. Williams gave me."

Autumn's heart skipped a beat. "Ball? What ball?"

Patience fell silent, red seeping into her features as she looked away.

"You were at one of Hortense's balls again? I thought I told you never to—"

"This is my point precisely!" Patience lurched back. "You are always telling me what to do and what not to do. I am your sister, not your daughter."

"We have no mother; therefore, it is my job to protect you and fill the role of one."

"I am twenty years old!"

"Far too young to be dancing with men at a ball, I am afraid."

"Young? Most everyone I know is married! I am ashamed that I am not yet wedded or at least in the fashion of attending social events and outings. You know just as well as I do that one of us must find a man sooner or later. After all, you are twenty-six; your chances of love are growing slimmer by the day. What happens if we keep this up and we end up poor and on the streets like we were before? I am scared!"

Autumn's eyes narrowed. "Neither of us need a husband to thrive."

"I may not need one, but I want one!"

"Ridiculous."

"You are wrong."

"Wrong? About what exactly? The fact that marriage is an unstable foundation on which to build your future and that you are simply too immature to understand? I seriously doubt it."

"That, and... and all the joy you have kept me from experiencing my entire life! I have wanted to tell you this for a long time, and here it is—I am ready, ready to be my own person, ready to step outside this home and choose my own destiny for myself. Ready to fall in love, feel the wind in my hair, and dance around England and, one day, the world!"

Autumn sucked a mouthful of air down her throat and puffed up her cheeks. "I..." She lifted her hand to the plain golden ring on her necklace, running her fingers along the shiny rim. "No... I mean, absolutely not. This is ridiculous!"

"So, you are saying that you can achieve your dreams but I cannot?"

"No. I am saying that my dreams are to keep us safe and that yours are a fantasy. Honestly, Patience, I know that you think yourself grown up, but you are not."

"Maybe if you would let me hold a butter knife for once, I would be."

"That's enough. In fact, I don't want to hear another word on the subject of you leaving me again, do you understand?

"You never let me do anything."

"That is because I care about you more than anything in this wicked world and I only want what's best for you. For both of us." Autumn kept her tone calm against her sister's anger.

"What's best? All you care about is that boring house and preventing me from getting what I want!"

"Do not raise your voice at me. You are staying with me. I shan't discuss this nonsense any further."

Patience scrunched up her face and paced forward, pushing her sister out of the way as she left the kitchen.

"Patience, come back." Autumn threw out her arm, fingertips spread as her sister thundered upstairs. "Goodness…" Autumn slowly let her arm fall, her eyes sad. What was she going to do with that girl? How could Patience ever wish to go out into the world like that? Even after all these years, she still had so much to learn.

Autumn shook her head and headed for the stairs, ready to resolve the debate. She took the steps one at a time, the old wood creaking beneath her every movement. She reached the top and pushed open the bedroom door to find Patience messing up her pretty blonde hair by rolling around on their rosewood poster bed. It took up most of the room and there was only just enough space for the mirror, the dressing table and upholstered chair, the chiffonier, and a dressing screen. The muted wallpaper was marked with age and torn in places; once, long before Autumn and Patience had moved in, it had been adorned with bright birds perched across the walls.

Autumn sighed and stepped in, running her fingers along the rim of her sister's fragile mahogany box camera with its leather bellows, which was placed on the dresser.

She was used to dealing with Patience. Their short conflicts always ended the same, with Patience moping around the house, a frown on her face, before bouncing back to her usual energetic self. Like the day Autumn had forbidden her from going to the spring festival. Patience had whined and protested for a few hours before feeling better when they went out for a picnic. This time would be no different.

"Listen, Patience," Autumn seated herself on the bed, sinking into the straw-filled mattress, and folded her hands in her lap.

"I'm tired of listening," Patience let out a groan and buried her face into a pillow, her arms perpendicular to her body.

"Goodness, would you act your age for once?"

Patience held her head up with her messy hair covering her eyes. "How do you expect me to act my age when you don't let me do anything?"

Autumn shook her head, catching sight of the hairbrush next to the candlestick on the chiffonier. "Listen, Patience," she said again, concentrating on keeping her voice calm as she picked up the brush and ran her fingers over the soft bristles. "There are some things you simply aren't ready for."

"I'm not ready for anything in your eyes."

"I know it feels that way, but I'm only trying to protect you."

"I don't need your protection; I can take care of myself!"

Autumn gave a tight smile, setting the brush aside. "Look, one day everything will be in place and you shall be content. You'll have a home, an income, and a body unmarked by injury or illness! You will be so thankful."

"Content." Patience said the word as though it hurt her to speak it as she rolled off the bed and onto the floor with a thud.

Autumn stood and made her way to the door, resting one hand on the frame. "You had better ready yourself for our guests tonight. You don't want to be in this shape when Mr. Williams arrives," she said, attempting to inspire her sister to change her attitude. "You left your evening wear in the dresser. And please, dear, don't pull at the drawer handles so hard. They could fall and break your feet." She closed the door with a soft click and headed downstairs to finish preparing supper.

2

"Patience!" Autumn called out. Evening was drawing near and storm clouds lurked on the horizon. The soup bubbled on the stove and the cake waited in the oven.

Autumn hadn't seen her sister since their discussion earlier that afternoon and hoped Patience had improved on her behaviour. Had she been too harsh on her? Maybe a little. But what else could she have done? If anything were to happen to Patience, anything at all... well, Autumn would never forgive herself.

Upstairs, her sister's feet thudded against the floor and a door closed sharply. Patience's head emerged as she came bouncing down the stairs, her clean curls flying over her shoulders, her eyelids lowered and her lips pursed together.

Autumn lifted the lid of the pot; the fumes within billowed free in misty bursts of haze. *Patience will feel better after dinner,* she thought, *once she has had something good to eat and something soothing to drink.*

"It smells lovely," Patience neared the stove, inhaling with exaggerated motions, closing her eyes and fanning her nostrils.

"Patty, please be careful near the stove."

"Pish-posh!" She moved a few inches to the side and wiped her moist face with a sleeve.

"Look at you, getting your pretty dress dirty before supper."

"I don't care!" Patience flashed her teeth. "I am going to change into my yellow gown anyway. Don't you think that Mr. Williams will adore it?"

"I suppose. Not that it matters much."

"Don't be so dull, sister." Patience swatted her on the arm with a dishcloth.

Autumn pulled at the tip of her sleeve and glanced away, puffing air into her cheeks. "Patience," she began, arms shaky. "I know that you are still disappointed about earlier…"

Patience put her hands behind her back and smiled tiredly.

Autumn swallowed. "Despite our conflicting desires, I want you to know that you can live a content and even exciting life with me, even if that means staying here in Carlisle. Anyway, I… the point is, I wanted to give you this."

She turned to the table and picked up a thick, leather-bound book with dirty string tying mismatched papers together. "This is Mother's old scrapbook." Autumn pulled back the cover and flipped through the interior. "I removed all the pages and replaced them with fresh ones. It's yours now. You can use it to document the adventures we have in our new home together. I believe Mother would have wanted you to have it, given how creative you are. You could paste in all the pictures you take."

Patience accepted the book with no enthusiasm, tucking the heirloom under her arm without so much as a second glance. Then she said,

"Why don't you go and dress? I will mind the kitchen while you're gone."

Autumn nodded, disappointed but not objecting to her sister's guidance for once. She needed a break. And so, after a quick glance at the stove and a peek at the cake, she dashed upstairs before she could change her mind.

After she had changed, Autumn stepped out from behind the dressing screen to admire her clean outfit in the mirror, for once not noticing that the rim of the glass was speckled with flakes of rust.

I look quite presentable, really, don't I? She bit her lip and smoothed her hair with her hands. Most of the strands were pinned back into a thick knot. She examined her gown, the tight bodice a fringed floral design with gold trim and laces across the chest. The skirt, rose and green, was heavy with a thick train.

Yes, she decided, giving her nearly elbow-length white gloves an extra tug for good measure. *That will do nicely*. She pushed her lips together and touched the tiny silver balls on her ears, the only pair of earrings she owned.

"Autty, darling!" Patience's voice echoed in the wake of the loud knocking from the front door. "They are here! Hurry!"

"I'm coming!" Autumn called back, her hand to her mouth. Then she bent down to pick up her stained apron. As she hung it on a hook, a banknote slipped from the pocket, drifting to the floor like a falling leaf.

"Goodness!" She picked up the valuable paper, then opened a drawer and took out a large jar stuffed to the brim with an equal mix of pounds, shillings, and notes.

"Autumn!"

"Coming!" She placed the note in with the others and set the jar atop the dresser beside Patience's camera, tossed another log on the fire, and gave a last glance in the mirror, placing her gloved hands on her waist as she did so. Something was missing... ah yes, her comb. She opened a drawer and picked out a metal decorative piece with a brass maple leaf and slid it into the knot at the back of her head. *Perfect*. She turned and headed down the stairs.

"I'm going to change!" Patience thrust her apron at Autumn and handed her a spatula, brushing against her shoulder as she headed for the bedroom.

"Goodness me!" Autumn tossed the apron over a kitchen chair.

Smoke breathed from the edges of the closed oven in cloudy puffs. *The sponge cake!*

"Patience! Where are the oven mitts?" She pulled open drawers and began throwing various items from within across the countertops in a series of bangs and crashes.

"Don't know! Where did you leave them last?" Patience called from the bedroom.

"If I knew I wouldn't be asking you!"

Someone knocked at the front door.

"Pay-pay!" Autumn's eyes widened as she slammed a cabinet. "You didn't let them in?"

"Did you see my outfit? A rather nasty shade of blue and with several stains. I wouldn't have been caught dead in it!"

"Why didn't you change sooner?"

The knocking proceeded.

"I'll get it! I'll get it!" Patience flew down the stairs; half tumbling and half flying as she tied a messy bow on her fresh sunshine-yellow dress.

"But the mitts! Oh, the cake! It's burning!" Autumn opened the oven, the smoke within bursting free.

"Look in the closet!" Patience shouted over her shoulder.

"Of all the days!" Sure enough, the mitts were in the closet.

"I'm coming!" Patience ran with her shoes in her hands and a hairpin in her teeth. "I'm coming!" She skidded down the hallway, bumping smack into a wall. "Ow!"

"Be careful!" Autumn warned too late.

"I'm okay! Ouch... that hurt..."

Autumn slowed her pace as she lowered the hot tray onto the table. The cake was a bit crispy around one edge but, thankfully, not burned.

"Autty, come on!" her sister yelled.

"Okay, okay." Autumn closed the oven, took off the mitts, and hurried to the front door. "Patience your bow is a disgrace!" She caught hold of the ribbon as they dashed for the door together, Patience skidding and Autumn flying behind while retying the yellow ribbon, both a blur of motion.

They slid to a halt just behind the door, adjusted their posture, and, each catching a twinkle in the other's eye, burst into merry peals of laughter.

"They will hear us," Patience giggled and put her hand on her side, leaning over.

"Open—" Autumn tried deep breathing to subdue her glee. "Open the door," she laughed, searching for breath, glad that they were no longer arguing. She had always known her sister would get over her anger.

Patience filled her chest with air and turned the knob.

"Mr. Williams!" The sisters curtsied with red faces.

"Miss Everleigh. Miss Patience Everleigh." The handsome Mr. Williams bowed in the doorway. Behind him were his sister, Mrs. Glendale, and the Pickerlys.

"Mrs. Glendale." Autumn and Patience lifted the front of their dresses a little as they curtsied, speaking as well as they were able, given their heavy panting.

"Mr. Pickerly," Autumn smiled as she greeted him. She had never before seen the bearded man in anything other than his farm clothes. The fine suit he wore now made him rather elegant in his old age, despite the fact that several loose pieces of straw were caught to his black tailcoat.

As everyone entered, the sisters exchanged a glance with smiling eyes, the argument and burning sponge cake all forgotten. Their guests were here and had no idea of the chaos they had quashed just before the front door was opened.

"If only you could have seen the horizon!" said Mr. Williams as everyone enjoyed the warm soup, clinking spoons against their bowls while thunder throbbed in the night sky. The only light came from a pulsing candle on the dining room table, which was dressed with plates, glasses, and a pitcher of wine. The cake and grapes sat alongside a collection of teacups on saucers.

"Mr. Williams," said Patience, propping her chin on her hand and leaning toward the end of the table, where he sat. "Do tell me again about the waterfall."

He laughed and wiped his mouth with a napkin, leaving crumbs behind on his modest mustache. "At that time, we had spent the entire day climbing another mountain off the coast of Angola, a huge mountain mind you, much taller than any fragile cliff here in England. Once we reached the top, we had to hurry to pitch our tents before nightfall. You can't imagine my surprise when I awoke the next morning to the booming sound of water flowing near my ears."

"A waterfall!" Patience squeezed her fists together and tightened her arms, a smile illuminating her face.

"I got up so fast my foot caught on the tent flap, and the next thing I knew, I fell face first into the dirt. But that didn't stop me from drinking from the falls! Water as cold as ice and pure as gold."

Patience closed her eyes and inhaled with a deep sensation of wonder. "I can almost taste it now!"

"I don't suppose it's much different than the water we have here," said Autumn without looking up from her bowl.

"Quite the contrary!" said Mr. Williams. "This water is quite different, due to the higher altitudes, minerals, and jungle mist. Much cleaner, too. Shall I tell you next about my encounter with the mottled spine-tail bird?"

"Yes!" said Patience, leaning forward.

Autumn gave her sister a nudge and whispered, "Sit like a lady."

Mr. Williams chuckled. "It was the beginning of our third week in the jungle, and I had yet to spot the creature, who is... picture something like a hawk. Then, one morning when I was up long before anyone else, I heard it. And sure enough, there in the tree above my head perched the mighty bird. I moved with caution, being sure not to frighten the fellow, as I inched my way to the tree and began the climb. I was not but halfway up when I heard it..."

"Heard what?" Patience cupped her hands together, mouth wide.

"The hiss of a python."

Autumn almost choked on her soup. "Goodness!"

"What did you do?"

"Kept climbing, of course. After all, I had to retrieve *this*." And he pulled out a glossy brown feather from his pocket and extended his reward toward Patience.

"You didn't!" she marveled, accepting the feather and turning the soft bristles over in her palm.

"It's yours to keep. The news already got the story."

Autumn cleared her throat. "You gambled your life for a feather?"

"If 'gambling' is the word of choice you prefer, then technically speaking, yes. Yes, I suppose I did."

"But you could have died!"

"Ah, naturally. But therein lies the very point of adventure: a man must live a fulfilling life somehow."

"What's so wrong with the normal kind of living that everyone else participates in?" Autumn brushed at her bangs and took a bite of broccoli. Cold.

"Oh, sister, allow the dear man his adventure!" Patience shook her head and handed her the feather.

"Yes, allow the dear man his adventure," teased Mr. Williams. After seeing Autumn's frown, he added, "Although you are right, you know. My adventures are not always as… straightforward as others might prefer, but what is life without a little spice, hmm?"

"I suppose that depends on how you like your meat seasoned," Autumn lowered her eyelids before blushing at her own impertinence, as she handed the feather to Mrs. Glendale.

"Another good point; another excellent point!" Mr. Williams smiled again, this time at Patience.

His smiles at Patience had been the most consistent thing that evening. Could he be flirting with her? Autumn hoped not. Mr. Williams had always been a kind enough man, now that she thought about it. He brought them little treasures from his travels or surprised them with the occasional picnic in a meadow or an excursion to Perlyn Hall. There were smaller things, too; bright ribbons and small vials of perfumes. He often brought gifts for both the Everleigh sisters, but more often than not, they were gifts for Patience. He was probably just being polite, as every proper gentleman ought.

Regardless of his intentions, Patience always glowed with joy whenever she received a letter or package from him. She would stop whatever she was doing, take a deep breath and, at a slow steady pace, open the envelope to sink into the written contents.

Mr. Williams was fine, Autumn decided, so long as he didn't get too close or offer to take them on one of his crazy escapades. And if he ever did make a move for love, she would put an end to that without a moment's notice.

"What about you two?" Mr. Williams kept his gaze on Patience. "How is life at the Raven's Nest, working for my sister?

"Quite pleasant, indeed. Isn't that right, Autty?"

Autumn, mid chew, put her hand to her mouth and glanced around the table before swallowing.

"Very well," she mustered, knowing she had no choice but to say yes with Mrs. Glendale present, although she did speak the truth. "The children adore their literature and history classes." She tilted her eyes in Mrs. Glendale's direction, who gave her the usual weary smile. Autumn always made sure to go out of her way to make the kind lady happy. After all, Mrs. Glendale had been rather generous in hiring both the Everleigh sisters for work, with Autumn as a full-time governess for the eldest children and Patience as a nanny for the baby. Autumn even found the children's company welcoming, for it proved to be a snug little life. However, her days would soon be even better once she moved into the new house with Patience and opened her bakery!

"The infant, my niece, must love you very much, no?" Mr. Williams tilted his head at Patience.

"I think so." She nodded eagerly. "She seems to like me enough. It feels like I'm practically family."

"Ah, yes. Those who are like family are the second-best kind of people."

Patience tilted her head and cupped her hands together. "Why, who are the very best?" Her curiosity sparkled as she reached for her glass.

"Why, family of course!"

For some reason, Patience must have found the remark rather comical, for she spit the water in her mouth across the table, spraying poor Mrs. Pickerly's face and ruining the rest of the sponge cake. Autumn glared at her sister and handed the dripping guest a fresh napkin.

Patience pressed her lips together as her cheeks became pink, and she sat glancing around the table with watery eyes as her lingering giggles faded.

Mr. Williams gave a chuckle and winked at her before facing the rest of the party. "Mr. Pickerly, are you preparing to sell your vegetables at the market come next month?"

"Why, yes, we plan to take some of the overflow to town as soon as we are able."

"Well, then," continued Mr. Williams, "I have many plants back at Perlyn Hall. Beautiful vegetables. Courgettes, tomato, lettuce. I am away so often that we don't know what to do with the overstock. I'd be more than happy to send some on to you."

"Oh, no," Mr. Pickerly shook his head and shrugged at his wife, "We couldn't possibly—"

"It would be my pleasure." Mr. Williams raised his hand to silence him.

"Thank you. You're quite generous."

"Not at all." He set his glass down with a hard clink on the table.

"Autumn, isn't that wonderful?" Patience leaned over and gave a harsh whisper in her sister's ear.

"I suppose..."

At that moment the candle had run its course and went out, leaving the dinner guests in darkness.

"Goodness," Autumn said, resting her spoon against the interior of her bowl.

Mr. William's struck a match, the light illuminating his face in an eerie glow.

"I do say," he whispered in a deeper tone than usual as he grinned at Patience, "Something has overturned our camp."

Patience clasped her hands over her mouth as her voice peaked with joy. "A jaguar, perhaps? How jolly!"

Mr. Williams stood and nodded, waving the match around. "I do believe there is an oil spill." He moved to Patience and handed her the match, then took her free hand and helped her rise from the chair.

Autumn crossed her arms and let out a huff.

"Look," said Patience, bending down and waving the match along the floor. "Blood."

"Get behind me," said Mr. Williams, using a hand to guard Patience. "We mustn't make any sudden movements lest we become sustenance for the hungry jaws of the enemy."

The duo crept toward Autumn, who only hugged herself and looked straight ahead, refusing to take part in their game.

No one said a word. Autumn turned her head to the left, coming face to face with a smiling Mr. Williams.

"Goodness!" She unfolded her arms and scowled. "You are honestly the most impossible man I have ever laid my—"

He extended a hand, and she gave an exasperated roll of the eyes, accepting his offer with a grudge and rising to her feet.

Patience handed her sister the match. "Find the one who killed our most beloved."

Autumn raised her hand above her head and waved the match back and forth. "I see something."

"Where?" said Patience, quieter than before.

"Near the caves."

"Look out!" Mr. Williams blew out the match as the sisters screamed in delight. All went silent. Autumn squeezed her hands into fists, a smile forming across her lips as she waited for Mr. Williams to guide their next move.

"That is enough, Clarence." Mrs. Glendale said in the dark, voice trembling.

"Is it?" His face appeared near the sisters as he struck another match. "Then I suppose we will never find out how the fearsome jaguar killed your dear uncle."

Autumn, still smiling, examined Mrs. Glendale, who lifted a hand to clean the tears shining on her cheeks.

"Mrs. Glendale, are you well?" Autumn questioned, cocking her head.

"Fine, fine," she sobbed, lips trembling.

Both sisters raised their brows as Mr. Williams gave his sister's hand a squeeze. "I know, darling. I miss him, too."

Mrs. Glendale refused to look her brother in the eye.

Autumn puffed air into her cheeks and turned away from the scene, not wanting to seem rude by staring. She found two fresh candles, which she lit and placed on the table. *Poor Mrs. Glendale must be afraid of the dark.*

"Patience, if you could remain standing." Mr. Williams let go of his sister's hand and approached her. She nodded, giving her pinned-up golden hair a brush with the hands.

Autumn took her seat, helping herself to some more wine with an elegant sweep of her arm.

"It occurs to me," said Mr. Williams in his normal voice. "That I made a commitment." He ran his fingers through his long sideburns and leaned back on his heels. "A commitment to see the world."

Autumn adjusted her overskirt, fluffing it out so it curved around the side of her chair before she folded her hands in her lap and leaned her head a little to the left, smiling.

"As you are all aware, I have succeeded in visiting many countries, which, thus far, have each been most agreeable, with the recent honour of visiting both Africa and Spain during this past year. Despite these small achievements of visiting with other nations of my wishing, I have yet to behold the honour of seeing the remaining continents on the list, which is why I have made the recent decision to embark on a world tour, set to begin course within the coming winter months."

Patience, overcome with delight, slapped his arm. "A world tour!" She glanced at her hand and pulled it back to her side.

Mr. Williams ran his hands though the top of his thick brown hair and turned to face Patience, his Adam's apple quivering. "Yes. I would visit a good portion of Europe and Asia, along with North and South America, ending here in England all before this time next year." The man swallowed, cleared his throat and, with shaky legs, dropped to one knee.

Both sisters gasped in unison. Autumn shot up from her seat like a lightning bolt. Mrs. Glendale put a hand on her shoulder, directing her to sit. Autumn obliged, stomach churning.

"Patience, I have been besotted with you since the moment I laid eyes on your precious heart. So much so that, when I wasn't traveling, you were all I could think of. In fact, even when I *was* traveling, you filled my waking thoughts. I became lost, physically and emotionally, without your company. You are a wonder; unlike any woman I have ever met. You are smart and caring, and you have an unfading joy that fuels your every movement." He sniffed, wiping a tear from his eyes. "I have not seen such joy in a long, long time..."

Autumn's heart thundered. "Mr. Williams," she gave a harsh whisper which he did not acknowledge. "Patience!"

Her sister flashed Autumn a sideways glance, face aglow.

Mr. Williams wiped his eyes again. "I believe that, last year, I promised you I would one day take you with me on my travels. You waited, so patiently, Miss Patience. You waited for me to come back time and time again, and so I ask you, as I prepare to set foot on my next adventure... Will you, Patience Adriana Everleigh, not only join me on this world tour, but also do me the honour of joining me in my life by becoming my faithful bride?" He took her hand in his.

"Mr. Williams!" Autumn stood, shoving her chair to the side, the wooden legs squeaking along the floor. "My sister is not interested in your proposal."

Mrs. Glendale set her hand on her shoulder again, but Autumn wrenched free in fury.

"Yes," Patience said with emotion, keeping her eyes on Mr. Williams. "Yes, of course I will marry you!"

His face broke into relief as he let go of her hand, produced a ring, and slipped it over her finger.

No. No. No. Autumn's arms started to shake as her teeth chattered. No. This wasn't happening. This couldn't be real. What about the house? Their future? Keeping her sister safe? Her promise...

Autumn gripped the edge of the table, her head growing dizzy. "Patience, what on earth are you doing?"

"Autumn, it's all right. It's... it's wonderful!"

"No." She paced forward, closing her fingers over sister's hand. "No, it is not all right. Give that ring back this very instant."

"Get away!" Patience pulled free.

Autumn stamped her foot and flipped her hands to the sky, gritting her teeth at Mr. Williams. "Take it back from her."

"Miss Everleigh, I—"

"Take it!" Autumn's face grew paler by the second as she swallowed and clutched her throat in pain.

"I won't give it to him!" Patience backed against the wall and concealed the ring with her right hand. "You can't make me!"

"Miss Everleigh, let me take full responsibility for surprising you with this proposal," Mr. Williams said calmly.

"I have no desire to hear anything you wish to say in this moment."

"Let him speak!"

"That is enough, Patience. Go to your room."

"I won't! You can't tell me what to do anymore!"

Autumn clenched her jaw. How dare Patience treat her this way? She was embarrassing her in front of everyone. Patience had no idea what it was like to be on the other side, to desire safety, to witness loss.

"Please, Patty. Go."

Patience didn't move.

Autumn faced the table. "Ladies and gentlemen, please excuse my terrible rudeness, but I am afraid our dinner must be cut short this evening."

Mr. Pickerly stood, tapping his wife on the shoulder. "The meal was lovely, thank you so much. You are a wonderful cook."

"Why thank you," Autumn nodded, puffing her cheeks. The elder couple took each other by the arm and excused themselves.

"Brother—" Mrs. Glendale dabbed the corners of her mouth with a napkin.

Mr. Williams looked at Autumn with furrowed brows and saddened eyes. "Miss Everleigh, allow me to explain myself."

"Mr. Williams. I am requesting that you leave our home. Please be so kind as to oblige me. If you do not, I am afraid I may be forced to call for the police."

His mouth quivered open as his eyelids lowered. "Forgive me." He gave a last glance at Patience and stormed out of the dining room, footsteps thundering.

"Autumn, I refuse to let you do this!" Patience cried.

"Silence, Patience." Autumn followed the guests to the door. "Thank you for coming." She curtsied to the farmers and Mrs. Glendale. "Mr. Williams." She made a tight smile, nodding, as she gestured towards the door.

He tipped his hat and opened his mouth once more but said nothing.

Once the door was closed and the sisters were alone once again, Autumn grabbed Patience roughly by the arm and pulled her upstairs.

"How dare you!" She tore into the lit bedroom dragging a frazzled Patience behind.

"I am sick and tired of you choosing how I live my life!" Patience wrenched free of her sister's grasp and lost balance, falling across the bedspread.

"You selfish child!" Autumn kicked the door shut as she shouted. "Every. Single. Day. Of. My. Life! Has been spent caring for you, protecting you and it has all led to what—this? Well, I won't have it! I swore to myself that I would do everything in my power to be here for you and keep us both from harm. I struggled and laboured, and I am not about to go back on that promise!"

"Mr. Williams is better family than you'll ever be!"

Autumn's heart throbbed like an open wound.

"And that's even worse!" she answered with as much courage as she could muster, letting her view fall to the crackling fireplace. "Of all the people who could possibly care for you, that insincere man is the last. Honestly, stop and think for but a moment! Mr. Williams spends every penny he makes on his travels! Do you really want to rely on a man who could become destitute at any given moment? Throwing his life into chaos all for the delight of temporary pleasures? He is bound to fall into the same trap our—" Autumn stopped, her voice weak with emotion. She opened her mouth a crack and took short, quivering breaths as her body shook. This was all too much. She couldn't go on any longer. She had to end this. Now.

She spoke gently, now. "Patience, you just have to trust me. Come here." She held out her arms, ready to embrace her sister so they could go on with their life.

Patience drew back, eyes wet and fiery. "How do you expect me to trust you when you do not trust me? This is my only chance for freedom. My one chance to live a life where I can make my own choices, see the world, take photographs just as I have always dreamed, and never again hear you say the word *no!*"

Autumn put her hands to her bare neck, bumping against her dangling necklace. "Listen to yourself talk! I am not even convinced you love him!"

"Love him? Of course I love him! I have spent nearly every minute thinking of the man for the past fifteen months! He is everything I have ever wished you were to me and more. But of course, you wouldn't know. Every time I try to share my dreams with you, you crush them into a thousand tiny pieces!"

Autumn shook her head violently, her eyes on the floor.

"You will regret this. This will break you, Patience. If you marry him, you will lose everything we have built together. This mistake will haunt you for the rest of your life, and you know it just as well as I do... We have a special connection, and whether you want to realise it or not, I love you more than anything in this fragile, decaying world, so much so that it would shatter me to sit by and watch as you plunge into dark waters that I know you will drown within. Don't you see?" Autumn cleaned her eyes with one finger, dabbing the corners and closing her lids.

"You are trying to manipulate me." Patience hissed, and Autumn caught a suggestion of sadness in her tone.

"No. I am trying to care for you. Mother wouldn't have wanted this. You know she would have wanted us to remain together."

"I know she would have wanted me to be happy!"

"And you can be happy. Happy with me!"

"No, I can't, Autumn. A life isolated from the world is hardly a life worth living!"

"A life isolated from you is hardly a life worth living!"

"Then you will have no choice in my absence but to end yours."

Autumn's eyes widened; the words stung as if they had pierced the skin.

"Give me that ring." She advanced.

"No!"

"I will not sit by and watch you throw your life away! You will stay with me. I will take care of you as I always have, and we can live in our new home, together forever, and I will keep you safe!" Autumn grabbed her sister's hand.

"Enough talk of that ridiculous house!"

"It's not ridiculous. It's called life!"

"If that's life, then I don't want a wretched part of it!" Patience jerked out of her sister's hold and stumbled back. She shook her head, her gaze falling to the dresser and the jar of Autumn's savings. She picked it up.

"Patty, put that down this instant!" Autumn tried to grab at her sister's hands, but Patience held the container up and out of reach.

"I am marrying Mr. Williams, and nothing you can ever do will stop me!" Patience made a swift movement and thrust the jar and its contents over Autumn's head and into the crackling fireplace. The glass exploded, shattering into smoky flames.

"There!" Patience smiled wickedly with defiance.

Autumn's face crumpled as she stared, eyes locked on the red flames devouring her precious savings. Her years of hard work.

"Autumn?" Patience's voice cracked.

Autumn faced her sister, face lit with sorrow as anger swept through her body. "If you refuse to listen to me, then I will just have to make you understand!" Autumn shoved Patience to the ground and lifted the heavy wooden camera off the dresser.

"Ow!" Patience lay on the floor and pulled her hair away from her eyes, gazing up at her sister.

Autumn's entire body shook with unbearable sobs as she lifted the camera high above her head and, with one fell swoop, slammed the frame into the dresser. Wood splinters flew from the wreckage.

"Autumn, no!" Patience cried, throwing out her arm hopelessly.

Autumn lifted the expensive camera a second time as tears flowed over her face, bleeding down her neck and embroidering her collar.

"This is for your own good!" She collided the box against the dresser again and again, sending wood chips flying across the room with every hit until the camera was smashed to pieces.

"Ohh-ohh!" Patience wailed, stumbling to her feet and crying. She blundered, unbalanced, as she brushed past her sister, the breeze rustling against her hot face.

Autumn dropped the misshapen camera as her legs collapsed under her. She fell to her knees, unable to stand, with her face bent over and head touching the cold floor.

Patience let herself out in tears, shaking as she entered the hall. The door slammed shut behind her.

3

February 15, 1866

Dear Diary,

This most awful thing in the world has happened. I'm shaking as I write this and I can hardly hold the pen, but I must write it down. To stay strong for Mother and for Patience. I will share my heartbreak on these pages and I will take care of them as best I can.

I knew something was really, truly wrong when I heard the front door slam. I wanted to bury my head in my pillow and shut out the world and weep and weep but I couldn't. I had to comfort my sister.

"Don't worry, Pay-pay," I told her. I held her tightly. "Everything will be all right. You'll see." I tried to believe the words I spoke. Perhaps I did. Everything had always been all right, even if there were bad days.

My father had come home that afternoon with his pocket watch dangling from his suit, the cravat loose around his neck, and eyes dark and bleary. He looked as he always had whenever he lost a job or owed money to the bank. This happened so often that I barely took any notice.

I knew Papa gambled. He loved us but he also risked any and every-thing he had. Sometimes he risked things he did not have. We never stay in the same home for longer than a few months. We are a disgrace to society. But we were together and that was what truly mattered.

But, yesterday... oh, yesterday! Everything was different and then everything changed forever.

When our father came home defeated, he usually did his best not to show it. He would wash his face, embrace and kiss us all and, if I was lucky, dance around the room with me. Papa danced better than all the dancers in England. If you gave me the chance to do anything, anything in the entire world, I would choose to dance with my father.

Sometimes he did win in his gambles. Then he would come home with his pockets stuffed full of sweets or toys. Once he brought home a kaleidoscope. Our favourite treats were crispy brown squares of peanut brittle wrapped in paper, which we would eat with tea. On a bad day, he would mumble to himself until sunrise. Then the next adventure would begin.

"And that's why I married him," my mother told me countless times, "because of the adventure in his soul!"

I agreed with her. I have always loved the danger and excitement sur-rounding my father.

Mama loved him so much; I could tell by the way she treated him. Always gentle and sweet. Never once harsh or unkind, at least not while I was around. That's why my heart clenched with fear when I heard them. They had never fought before, not ever.

"Why are they shouting?" Patience asked. She pushed her face deep into my chest.

I didn't know what to tell her. She's still so young. Of course, they were arguing about money. I heard 'payment' and 'debt' but I could understand little else.

"Oh," I spoke brightly to her, as if the argument was a game that would soon end. "Don't worry. Papa is just upset that he lost in his business today."

Patience let go of me and hugged her knees to rock back and forth. "Do you think you and I shall have to shine shoes on the streets?" She looked at me with her sweet brown eyes.

"Why, of course not. Papa will always find a way to take care of us; don't you worry, my darling," I said, squeezing her.

Patience returned the embrace and hopped off the bed. "Maybe I could help." She produced a few shiny coins from the drawer—halfpennies.

"That's very kind of you," I cooed. "But Papa would never take your money."

She nodded, eyeing our bedroom door before replacing the valuables for safekeeping.

"Besides," I gave her a nudge, "he promised, remember?" I closed my eyes and remembered his words: 'Don't you worry, my dewdrop,' Papa had told me last year, when were forced to leave yet another home, 'I promise I will always be there for you and your sister.'

And he had kept his word. If there was one thing Papa had never done, it was break a promise he had made to me. Like the day he agreed to buy new thread and beads for my embroideries, but it started to rain. Papa went out anyway, risking getting wet all to avoid disappointing me.

"You don't understand!" His voice downstairs made me flinch now as my thoughts were interrupted. How dare he yell at Mother like that? Why couldn't he be calm, like he usually was?

"I want to understand!" Mama's frail voice shouted back, if you could call it shouting. My mother never sounded truly angry; her heart was too soft.

"If I don't find a way to pay them, it will be the end of me!"

"We shall find a way!" My mother's face blossomed in my mind. Her harsh breaths and trembling voice told me tears were flowing down her cheeks.

"Well," I locked eyes with Patience. I couldn't let her listen in on the argument any longer; she was only a child. "Let us do something to pass the time. Why don't we bake?"

"Oh, yes!" Her face cracked into a lovely smile.

I stood from the bed and pushed the door open with caution so as not to disturb the arguing below and tiptoed into the hall. My parents were silent, now. Had they heard us? No.

We reached the stairs and made our descent. We had to walk on tiptoes and test for creaky wood. I lifted one foot and put a hand to my ear, paused, stepped, and beckoned for Patience to follow.

Something hit a wall below. I froze, heart pounding.

I remembered my father's words: 'I promise I will always be there for you and your sister.' This comforted me, so I held Patience by the hand, and together we entered the kitchen.

"What shall we bake?" she asked.

"Peanut brittle! To cheer Papa."

We set to work.

"Easy now." I guided her hands as she dumped a cup of sugar into the saucepan. I went to the cabinet to get the peanuts, finding none. "Pay-pay, have you seen the peanuts?"

"I took them upstairs yesterday."

"You and your stomach," I laughed and kissed her on the head. "I will get them. You keep stirring the mix." And off I went, back to the stairs.

Papa entered the room below as I made the climb. I stopped halfway up the steps to crouch down and watch.

"Don't do this!" Mama begged. Her face was wet with tears, just as I had imagined.

"I'm worth more dead than I am alive," he groaned, slamming a fist into the wall. I jumped.

"I don't care if we have to work ourselves through hell to provide for our daughters! I just want to help you."

"The girls..." my father's eyes went dark, and he wiped his face with one hand. "This is for the best." He reached for the door to the room that was his study and flung it open with such force that the wood collided with the wall within.

"No!"

I couldn't get a glimpse of my father, but there were very loud crashings coming from his study.

Mama covered her mouth. "Mr. Everleigh, no!"

I couldn't recall anyone ever sounding more frightened than she did in that moment.

"Don't do this!" my mother begged, her voice throbbing as she rushed to the door, only to have Papa prevent her from entering. "Please!"

He muttered something I couldn't hear and pushed the door against Mama's weakening strength.

"Tell them yourself!" she cried.

Tell who what? My heart seemed to freeze inside my chest, a chill spreading throughout my body like a flourishing flame.

The door slammed shut with Papa alone inside.

And then... and then... just a moment later came a loud, sharp bang! My heart shattered at the sudden sound. Everything went silent. Mama sank to the floor as anguished tears flowed down her face.

Then she looked up at me. The tears flowing down her pretty face scorched my soul. I wanted to ask her what had happened, but I knew.

An awful sickness spread through my stomach. My hands were cold and numb as I reached for my mother. This must be a game. A trick. A joke, perhaps. He couldn't be...

Just as I wondered what to say to Mother, two feet pattered in behind me.

"What's happening?" Patience whispered. "Where's Papa?"

Mama let out a painful wail. I didn't say a word. Patience hurried over and squeezed me. I returned her embrace.

4

Mr. Williams is better family than you'll ever be!

Her sister's cruel words rang through her head as Autumn trudged down the dirt path from her home the next morning. The wind tousled her hair, the long strands that had come loose kissing her face in wispy lashes.

How could Patience say something so devastating? Hadn't Autumn given her more than she could ever desire? After all, not everyone had a sister to nurture and care for them as she did. Not only that, but Patience was willing to throw away everything they'd built together, everything they'd worked to gain for themselves and for each other. The joy and love, the days working together and evenings spent giggling... gone.

Autumn had always thought their bond meant more than anything in the world to Patience. It certainly did to her.

She rubbed her sore eyes as she walked along. She hadn't slept a minute that night. She'd wept until the tears ran dry and her soul could shake no more.

Patience was a fool. And if Autumn knew anything it was that she wasn't going to let her go through with this marriage, not when they were so close to a house of their own. To real independence! If Patience refused to cooperate, then she would go to the source of the problem. She strode with firm resolve toward the Raven's Nest to speak with Mr. Williams directly.

Autumn glanced down at the box she carried under her arm, filled with the charred coins from the fire. The notes had been burned up by the flames; however, every coin was salvageable, even if there weren't many.

The loss of almost all of her savings stung. It stung badly. She was practically back where she had started. She should never have kept the jar where her sister could reach it. Patience was rather ghastly for doing such a wretched thing! But yet, she herself was just as ghastly for destroying the camera.

She could always save more money, but she could never save for another Patience.

The Raven's Nest was a large old estate, both grand and pretty, set in a garden as large as a park. The front of the property gave way to open lawn and cobblestone paths surrounded by trees, creating protection from the heat come summertime and the wind in winter.

The manor itself stood three stories high, built from pale grey stone and showing off nearly forty individual white-rimmed windows on all sides, plus half a dozen chimneys and an assortment of slanted rooftops.

Autumn hurried through the walkway where pecking chickens were eating grain and entered through the servants' quarters to find a warm combination of fragrances tempting her senses. Eggs, tea, bread rolls, and ham were being prepared for the Glendale family. Despite herself, her stomach rumbled.

Autumn took the box out from under her right arm and switched it to her left as she stepped into one of the many halls of the home.

"What did you dream about?" came a child's voice from the dining room. "I dreamed I was an officer in war fighting the—"

"That's nothing!" another voice interrupted. "I dreamed I was Lady Elenway, daughter of the duke, with you and Mary tending to my every need!"

Autumn smiled at hearing the happy voices and stopped by the half-opened door to peek in.

The three older Glendale children—Hazel, Francis, and Mary-Elizabeth—sat at one corner of the long table, alone as usual. Mr. Glendale was far too busy operating the *Daily Post* and Mrs. Glendale was near her kin only on the rare occasion. Autumn felt this quite the pity for they really were lovely children.

"Mind that you don't spill, now," said a maid, wiping breadcrumbs from Mary-Elizabeth's mouth.

Still smiling, Autumn turned and went on her way down the hall, hurrying to find Mr. Williams so she could speak with him before she was needed in the schoolroom.

"Excuse me," she asked a nearby servant when she reached the formal entry of the home. It was a grand space with paintings on the walls, white pillars, and a staircase adorned with carvings of flowers. "Have you seen Mr. Williams this morning?"

"I have received word that he left for Perlyn Hall at dawn. You shall have better luck writing to him."

Blast.

"Mr. Williams is present," came a voice from behind her.

Autumn turned to face the staircase as Mr. Williams himself descended. He held a jacket in his arms and wore a grey waistcoat that met his red cravat with a tiny blue jewel. He trotted down the steps much like a show horse giddy at winning a ribbon.

The servant bowed.

"Mr. Williams." Autumn curtsied, a shiver consuming her body.

He nodded, face solemn.

Autumn stared at him, tears forming in her eyes. She hadn't meant to become emotional. She just wanted Patience back; that was all.

Mr. Williams took a glance at the ceiling and wrung his hands. "Miss Everleigh, if I may have the honour of conversing with you over a cup of tea...?"

She gave a swift, sharp nod of agreement.

Mr. Williams set his shoulders and paced down the hall, turning his head behind every so often as he walked as if to make sure she was still following him.

Neither said a word. Autumn followed obediently, pressing her hands against her stomach to quell her churning belly.

They soon entered the sitting room, which happened to be Autumn's favourite space in the home. It possessed a ceiling-high window that made the room bright and pleasant all year round.

"Please, sit," Mr. Williams directed her to a white-and-yellow striped couch.

She obliged, setting the box beside her. Then she folded her hands in her lap and made herself as comfortable as she could despite her burdens.

Mr. Williams seated himself in the armchair across from Autumn, set his jacket to the side, and said to the servant at the door, "A pot of tea for us, if you would be so kind."

"Of course, sir." The servant nodded and left.

Autumn sat motionless, blinking at Mr. Williams with a teary gaze of betrayal. She knew she wasn't making him very comfortable, but this situation was his fault to begin with.

"Miss Everleigh if... if I may have the first word?"

Her lips parted as she touched her teeth together. She did not answer.

Mr. Williams shifted in his seat and drew in a light breath. "I want to apologise for surprising you with the proposal last night." He ran his fingers along his mustache. "I should have consulted with you first, and I cannot imagine the grave shock you must have experienced. I was... thoughtless, in my excitement. I apologise for that oversight."

"A very grave shock indeed," she answered truthfully, nodding, "I shan't forget it."

He nodded, rolling his neck once. "Can you ever forgive me?"

Her muscles tightened as she pulled at the sleeve of her dress. "Forgiveness shall come only upon one's persuasion, assuming you have an inkling of the morality of a somewhat righteous man."

"What kind of persuasion are you suggesting?"

"To change your mind about the feelings you have proclaimed for my dear sister."

"I cannot change what is beyond my control."

"No, but you can shape your actions from this moment forward, and every moment thereafter."

The servant returned, set a tea tray on the low table in the centre of the room, and went about filling the cups.

Autumn stood, her voice urgent, as she shooed the server out of the way.

"I shall help myself, thank you." She wrestled the pot out of his hold. The baffled servant backed away, giving Mr. Williams a stray glance.

Autumn used a spoon to stir some sugar into her cup and returned to her seat. The servant approached the teapot with caution and poured tea for Mr. Williams.

Autumn blew on her steaming beverage and inhaled. The fresh ginger fragrance exhilarated her nostrils. Delicious.

Mr. Williams took a sip of his tea as the servant took his leave, then faced the bookshelf, as if to gather his thoughts. Turning back to Autumn, he said,

"Miss Everleigh, would you provide clarity as to your objections with the arrangement between myself and your sister?"

"Objections? Why, certainly, for I have many! The first being that you indulge in risky travels while throwing away more money than I ever could comprehend spending in a single sitting. And while I have yet to find flaws in your character, aside from your selfish outlook on life, I am sure that you would, in fact, make most any plain woman happy. But not Patience. She may enjoy the temporary pleasure of elopement until she experiences the severe consequences of leaving me behind, giving way to a life of... calamity."

"I did expect you to be… pleased, at my proposal. Grateful, even."

"Grateful, indeed! I am, rather, deeply troubled by your surprise advancements toward her." She tried to contain the fire inside.

"Well. I am, after all, raising your family name out of poverty. I doubt any other man of my class would dare consider compromising his public image in such a way."

"Do you consider this marriage a favour you grant?"

"I consider you blessed."

"Sir, my sister and I are not in poverty."

"Then what are you in?"

"The presence of a prideful man. Being rich doesn't give you authority over my sister or myself."

"No?"

"No. Not as far as I'm concerned." She folded her arms and then dropped them to her side. "You stand on a platform that could collapse at any moment. You spend every penny you make on travelling, and it will take only one painful endeavor to bring about your downfall."

"I've noticed that you disapprove of my travels."

"And do you live life that way, Mr. Williams?"

"In what way?"

"A way where everything always works out for you?"

"Are you suggesting I am of ill character?"

"The worst kind of ill character." Autumn set her beverage down with a clink and fumbled around in her bag until she produced a piece of paper. She leaned forward and set the page on the table.

He stood, still holding his cup, as he approached the coffee table and lifted the paper.

"This is a contract I have drawn." She watched him as he scanned the page. "You would agree to my terms and sign at the bottom, vowing to never again seek affection or any association of romance with my family for as long as you shall live."

Mr. Williams did not reply. He continued reading the document. She opened the box beside her. "Of course, I cannot expect that you would agree without gaining something in return, so I offer you in exchange all the savings I have, along with two years of cooking services to be at your disposal." She swallowed, holding down the urge to cry.

Mr. Williams gave a quick glance at the coins, face softening. "Miss Everleigh. I know you are close with your sister."

"Incredibly. I have cared for her as if she were my own child."

"And I am not trying to take her from you. Quill?" he rose his voice, using a tone that alerted the servant, now waiting by the door, to his request. A moment later the servant brought him pen and ink.

Autumn swallowed at the lump in her throat as Mr. Williams bent down to the low table and began to write.

She turned her head, trying to read the upside-down text, but she could make out only a few stray words: care... love...

When at last he had finished, he lifted the paper. "While I cannot sign the contract you have drawn, I can sign this."

Tears came to Autumn's eyes.

The man reached into his pocket and pulled out a pair of spectacles. He read aloud what he had written.

"I, Clarence D. Williams, hereby swear to care, protect, nourish, and love Patience Everleigh as my best friend, greatest desire, and love of my life, to never put her in harm's way and always set her needs above all else, including my own."

He set the sheet back on the table and signed under his text, handing the paper to Autumn.

She shook her head, staring at the words.

"That's not good enough." She wiped her eyes, setting the piece aside and trying to clean the loose tears smeared across her fingers.

"Here." Mr. Williams extended a handkerchief to her, but Autumn refused to accept the gesture.

"Nothing you do will be good enou—" she choked, struggling to finish her sentence. Her face must have been an embarrassment to behold, but what did it matter? She was about to lose her sister!

"N-nothing you do will ever be good enough, unless you take the disgraceful ring back and pretend that she has ceased to exist." And Autumn burst into tears, covering her face with her dress and shaking. "Please! I am begging you, Mr. Williams. I will do anything. I'll give you all I possess if you will only do as I have requested." She erupted into a nasty fit of coughing, and he again offered his assistance.

"I don't want your help." She bent in half as she tried to subdue her coughs in her elbow.

"What on earth is happening?" Mrs. Glendale rushed into the room wearing a muted dress and a hat decorated in white ribbons and bird feathers. "I thought you had left."

"Sister," he stood, meeting her halfway and taking her hands in his.

"Good morning, Mrs. Glendale," Autumn rose on shaky legs but quickly lost her balance, collapsing back on the couch with a sniffle.

"My goodness, child, are you quite well?" She sat down next to Autumn and used her own handkerchief to clean Autumn's face. Autumn didn't like this much, but felt too exhausted to complain.

Mr. Williams stared at Autumn, his expression pitiful. She stared back, thinking that he must feel quite sorry about how truly blanched she looked. This was all his fault.

"Miss Everleigh, if I may proceed to convince you otherwise, in hopes of softening your opinion toward the match between myself and your sister, I think it best that you know that I lost my older brother to the grave when he was but ten years of age."

Autumn's lips parted as a chill went down her spine. She hadn't heard this story before. Nor did she care to.

Mrs. Glendale stood, her body shaking as she joined her brother, placing a hand on his arm, chin trembling as her eyes grew wet.

Mr. Williams went on, "He was a wonderful boy, despite teasing me every now and then..."

Mrs. Glendale gave him a nudge.

"Regardless of these critiques, I loved him, loved him dearly. And after the day he passed, we both," he squeezed his sister's arm, "experienced terrible pain. I thought at times I may never feel truly happy, truly fulfilled, in all my life. That is, until I met Patience, nearly fifteen years later." He let go of his sister and approached Autumn, who eyed him as if he were ill and pulled both feet up onto the couch, hugging her legs and inching back.

"May I?" He sat down beside her, offering his open palms. She wasn't quite sure why, but she allowed him to take her hands. "Miss Everleigh, I want you to understand that there is one thing I would never do and that is bring harm to someone who brings me joy. I want Patience to be my wife more than I want anything else. I love her. She is my love, and I am just as capable as any other good man out there. If there's anything I know, it's that I will do everything to assure her security and safety. My love will last. It will be stronger than time itself and as unbreakable as the bond of a father and child."

Autumn shook in frantic motions. "And that's just where you've got it wrong." Her voice cracked. "Love isn't enough to assure someone's safety. I am dreadfully sorry about your brother, and I know the pain you experienced was terrible. But believe me, Patience will never be able to replace your loss."

"She is not a replacement. Our union is the start of a new chapter in life. In both our lives."

"It is not the start of a life but rather the end of one! Have you no care in the world that you are damaging the relationship we have? This will crush her. You have no idea the complexity of the bond we have built. She is all I have.

"You are a kind man, that I do not doubt. But you have your ways, and I have mine, and I cannot trust you any more than I trust myself."

Mr. Williams let go of her hands and stood, running his fingers through his hair. "Then I am sorry."

"For what?" Autumn flipped her palms upward and cocked her head a little to the left.

"For being unable to grant your request."

"You still plan on pursuing my sister, despite my utmost desires?" asked Autumn and touched her teeth together, leaving her lips parted.

"Precisely." He made his eyebrows sag. "The last emotion I want to bring you is grief. But I do not consider my actions unjust."

Autumn exploded in another fit of sobs. "You are even more selfish than I thought."

"That makes two of us." He ran his hand through his hair, eyes widening.

Autumn glanced at Mrs. Glendale, desperate for any backup. "And you?" She gestured to the woman, making her voice delicate. "Are you content with your brother marrying my sister, despite the... their differences?"

Mrs. Glendale, whose eyes were still damp, gave a brush at her brown hair and nodded. "If my brother has a chance of witnessing happiness again, then I can wish for nothing more. And I personally see your sister as... well. Like a member of my own family."

Autumn let her mouth fall open in shock, no longer caring to seem composed. Then she stood, took the contract, and stuffed it into her handbag.

"If neither of you have anything more to say, then this is where I bid my goodbyes. Mr. Williams. Mrs. Glendale." She bowed her head. "I appreciate your time."

"Don't be upset, my dear," Mrs. Glendale put a hand on her shoulder. "Every woman settles down and finds an eligible suitor eventually. I believe you will be thankful once you experience the wealth of the arrangement."

"Eligible...?" Her eyes welled with tears, and she marched out of the room, leaving Mrs. Glendale and her brother in the wake of her misery. Autumn found the staircase and lifted her skirts as she hurried toward the children's washroom. Finding the door, she entered with a sob. Her teary face stared back at her from the slim piece of mirror.

Autumn reached blindly for a bucket of clean water, and her hand hit a vase, sending the valuable item to the floor. It shattered into a hundred tiny pieces.

"Oh, no." She covered her face with her hands and lowered herself to the ground, eyes overflowing with tears. Her hands met the tiled floor, fingers bumping against the broken porcelain.

"Oh, no, no, no," she coughed, unable to stop shaking. She sniffed. She didn't deserve this. If only she had permission to stay here on the floor and never move again. However, she had the Glendale children to educate. And if she stayed here, someone would find out, and she would be out of a job.

So, having no other choice, Autumn stood to her feet and, after cleaning her eyes and dousing her red face with cold water, found a broom and dustpan to clean up the broken ornament. She wished she could run home and change her clothes, but she hadn't the time. Her dress was ever so crushed from where she had worried it in her hands.

"Autumn, are you well?" Hazel asked when Autumn entered the well-lit schoolroom.

"You look as though you have been crying!" Francis said as he turned to face her.

"Fran!" Hazel crossed her arms. "You needn't make her feel worse!"

"What?" He threw his hands in the air.

Autumn wiped her blotchy face and stumbled over to the stool she always sat in when she taught her classes. The children gathered around her like little sheep coming to their shepherd.

"Tell us what happened? Please," Hazel knelt and put a hand on Autumn's arm.

"Here." Little Mary-Elizabeth handed Autumn a wooden elephant.

She accepted the toy without giving it a glance and instead stroked the young girl's hair.

"Don't be afraid to tell us," said Francis. "After all, we only bite our enemies."

Autumn tried to smile. She would have loved to share her feelings with someone caring, but she couldn't burden the children. Besides, they had waited long enough to start school as it was.

"Let's see. In arithmetic yesterday we learned about the multiplication of seven," Autumn began with a cracked voice, fearing that she was about to cry again.

The Glendale siblings all exchanged glances and tilted brows but said nothing. They tiptoed to their spots and pulled out their study guides without so much as a word, a rarity which betrayed just how wretched their governess appeared.

Autumn's humour did not improve all the rest of the day. She found her thoughts wandering, and twice that afternoon she sat staring out the window, only to have one of the children pull her back into reality.

"Please don't tell Mrs. Glendale," Autumn begged with a shiver.

"You'll have to bribe me first." Francis rubbed his thumb and pointer finger together.

"Fran!" Hazel scolded. "We would never tell!"

"All too true," admitted Francis. "Mother doesn't listen much to us, anyhow!"

When the children had gone to the attic on break to play soldiers at war, Autumn sat in the schoolroom's cushioned window seat beside the red velvet drapes and wrote in her journal.

What to do? What to do?

Autumn's writing came out in awkward jumbles of stray sentences. Some words kept recurring: *destruction... ridiculous... savings... loss.*

"I can't lose her," she whispered, putting her head in her hands and blinking back tears. *I'm sure Patience didn't mean what she said*, she tried to reassure herself, sweeping a stray piece of hair back into place while clasping her teeth together. She wrote in her journal:

She doesn't know what she's doing. She is acting upon impulse. What to do?

What to do, indeed. Perhaps they could both move to the other side of England to get away from Mr. Williams! Not a bad idea, but Patience would never follow. She could get Mr. Williams to fall in love with someone else... no, not likely.

She turned back to her journal. The word *trapped* sprang out at her. That gave her an idea. She went to work, scribbling away as a weak smile formed on her face.

Patience and I are together, reading our favourite book under our parasols in the sun. Apple cider is bubbling on the stove inside, and we are both safe and secure. I am providing for her, and we live in my new home with the white-trimmed door. I have savings in the bank. And, best of all, I have dear Patty close by my side.

Autumn read the words describing a reality she certainly didn't have and the one she wished for the most. Yesterday that dream had been within her grasp, but now? Gone.

What would she do if she really could write the future into existence? First, she would write so that Mr. Williams and Patience weren't engaged. Or better yet, make them forget one another entirely. Then she would give herself as much money as she needed. Enough to never starve or go without fresh boots or clothing. And then the house... the beautiful, perfectly proportioned house for her and her sister.

Patience and Mr. Williams are separated. Both completely forget about the marriage.

She wrote and admired her work. If only it were that easy.

She clasped her head, dropping her journal to the floor. *I can write things into existence!*

The idea flourished. She could write. Not in her journal, but in a letter. She stumbled to her feet and collected her journal. She would write her way through this. She just had to commit the idea to paper. Writing would be the solution.

All Autumn had to do was write two letters. One addressed to Mr. Williams and the other to Patience, each announcing the end of their engagement. Of course, neither of the writings would be authentic, but no one needed to know that. Everyone would fall for her scheme so long as Autumn used particular care to make sure no one discovered her part in calling off the engagement.

Was tricking Patience wrong? Perhaps. But this was for her own benefit. Ignoring the problem would only do more damage.

When classes ended for the day, Autumn collected her things and said goodbye to the children, who begged her to stay and play. She told them she couldn't, not today, but promised to do so soon. After that, she headed downstairs, rushing to get home and begin work on her new plan.

"Goodness!" Autumn's boot slipped on the bottom step, sending her forward and sprawling across the entryway floor. Her box of coins, handbag, and journal went flying from her grasp.

"Honestly!" she grumbled, getting up and feeling her back with her hands. "Ow!"

"My word! Are you hurt?" Mrs. Glendale said, entering the space. Her eyes were wet.

"Fine, thank you." Autumn stood and shook out her skirt, face red.

Mrs. Glendale nodded and picked up the open journal. "You dropped this."

The red crept into Autumn's neck as she reached a hand out, but Mrs. Glendale didn't hand the book over. Instead, she eyed the open page.

"May I?" Autumn asked in a hurry, extending her hand. The woman obliged.

Autumn glanced at the entry with all her writings from that day and shut the cover, biting her lip. She collected her handbag and tucked the box under her arm.

"Miss Everleigh. I hope that you are not still thinking of separating my brother from his love. I understand that you are disapproving of the marriage, but there is nothing you can do about the collaboration. She has already said yes to the proposal."

"Ma'am, with all due respect, I shall continue to act with the purpose of caring for my sister."

From upstairs came a thundering of running feet and the shouting of the children.

Autumn and Mrs. Glendale faced the stairs as Mary-Elizabeth flew down the steps, tears glistening on her cheeks.

"Mistress Mary-Elizabeth!" someone yelled from above.

Mary-Elizabeth headed to her mother and wrapped both arms around her waist, burying her face in her mother's dress.

"Mary!" Mrs. Glendale lurched back, putting her hands above her head as her daughter held on to her midsection. "Do get away! Please!"

"Mistress Mary-Elizabeth!" Two plump maids with blazing cheeks came bouncing down the stairs, arriving on the scene. "We are so sorry, madam. We tried to stop her!"

Mrs. Glendale's arms shook as she exhaled in quick spurts.

"Mama, Francis called me an awful name!"

"Take her out of here," choked her mother, her face white.

"There, there, my love," crooned one of the maids as she lifted Mary-Elizabeth into her arms. "Let us go and get you something warm to drink." And she carried the crying child away rather briskly.

"Sincere apologies," said the other woman. She hurried to catch up to the retreating maid, and they bent their heads, murmuring to each other.

Autumn said nothing and stared at the sad sight of the vibrating Mrs. Glendale. The poor soul. She had never seen her employer so upset!

The older woman kept her eyes shut as she whispered gibberish under her breath.

"Well, good day, Mrs. Glendale—"

Mrs. Glendale blinked, opened her eyes, and focused on Autumn. "Miss Everleigh," she began, her voice a hoarse mutter, "I suggest that if you wish to remain under my authority, you stay out of the way of this marriage. You have yet to offend me, and we have no odds to address with one other. However, if you continue to agitate yourself over this proposal, I warn you that it will not sit well with me."

"I- I am so sorry. I didn't mean any harm."

"Do not be. It is not your doing. Now, please. Good day." She bowed her head, eyes swollen.

Autumn curtsied, then tucked her journal under her arm and walked away. She left the house quickly and, as she hurried along the path, she felt the fall breeze sweep across her hot face and flutter her skirt.

Never in all her life had she seen Mrs. Glendale so emotionally unstable. Of course, the woman had always been quiet as long as Autumn had known her, and she seemed rather lonely. She never went out of her way to spark conversation or to be the centre of attention, but this was a new level of disagreeable.

Autumn kicked at a stray pile of leaves as she walked along. Perhaps the woman missed her husband. After all, he was hardly around these days. Or maybe she, too, was a little sad that her brother was taking his next step in his life, which assured his greater absence.

Whatever the reason may be, Autumn decided she best be wary of speaking ill of the wedding or Mr. Williams around her. Especially after the lady's words of caution. Did she mean to threaten Autumn or merely state her opinion?

A single, vibrant orange leaf drifted from above and brushed her hair on the way to the ground. She stared at the leaf. The colour was so bright that it didn't quite fit in among the others, perhaps because the ones in the grass were already dead. Another leaf floated down and landed on the pile. It, too, had the sharper, deeper colour.

Autumn bent over, set down her things, and took both leaves in her hands. She turned them over, delighted that both were beautiful and unique pieces of nature, each so like the other.

"Both, in unison." She sighed with some comfort and found a nice little spot for the leaves to dwell in the sun together.

Autumn collected her belongings, and went on her way.

A raw silence greeted her when she passed through the front door of her house. Not the normal kind of silence, for birds still chirped in the trees, but an unusual silence between her and her sister. If Patience had returned home before Autumn arrived, she usually greeted her sister with frantic hugs and bounces before sharing something exciting that had happened. It was not so today.

Autumn walked into the sitting room, the click of her boot heels echoing. She paced the length of the room several times. Then she went up the creaky stairs and entered the bedroom to find Patience reading on their bed.

"Oh—"

Her sister gave Autumn one look, eyes red, snapped the book shut, and strode toward the door.

It hurt. They rarely argued, which made this worse. It had gone on far too long, and Autumn knew no way of bringing about immediate relief. Especially when Patience was the one in the wrong here. She had entered a proposal without thinking of her sister. She had escalated the argument and burned the money! Perhaps all she needed was a little coaxing. After all, they hadn't said so much as a word since last night. Since they'd each had time to process their thoughts, Patience might act differently.

"Well," said Autumn, putting her hand on the door to prevent her sister from leaving.

Patience gave a light shake of her head, causing her curls to slide over her shoulders as she put a finger under her lower lip, sadness glistening in her eyes.

"Well..." Autumn touched her teeth together. "Is there anything you'd like to say to me?" She stared at her dress, regretting her choice of words almost as soon as she'd spoken them.

"No, thank you." Patience swallowed, shoved past Autumn, and left.

Autumn squeezed her arms against her chest with fists facing up as she pushed her back against the door, closing it, and slid down the frame to weep on the floor.

She felt hopeless. Even if she could save Patience from Mr. Williams, they would never be as happy as they once were.

Eventually, Autumn lifted her aching body off the floor and made her way to her dressing table. She pulled out a fresh sheet of paper. She needed hope and had to start somewhere. Right now, that was by getting into the head of Mr. Williams.

"Dear Patience Everleigh," she muttered softly to herself, "I'm sorry to inform you that—"

Inform her of what? He found another love interest? Decided he no longer loved Patience? She stared out the window for some time before she penned the letter.

Dear Patience,

I regret to inform you that I no longer intend to marry you. I have met other people and realise that your class is so very far below my own. Miss Everleigh was right all along. I wouldn't marry you even if my own life depended on it. Please do not show your face in my presence ever again.

Yours pompously,

Mr. Williams

The letter needed work. A lot of work. She tore the paper to pieces and started fresh. Time went by as she attempted to master her craft. She wrote, shredded, and wrote some more.

By the end of the evening, she had completed the final draft.

My Dear Patience Everleigh,

I write this letter in my grief as I cannot bear speaking with you in person.

As hard as I try, I cannot deny my feelings or my deep affections toward you. You are indeed a worthy woman in every sense of the word.

While my feelings are stronger than I myself can comprehend, I realise I am the last man in the world who deserves to be called your husband. I live a life of unpredictability, and such a calling brings great risk. Risk that no well-tempered young lady such as yourself should ever be exposed to, not least by a man who loves her so very dearly.

You deserve safety, security, and predictably. After much careful consideration, I find that it would not only be selfish for me to go on with this marriage but also thoroughly unjust for your sake.

It is therefore, with a heavy heart, that I request you refrain from writing, calling upon, or speaking with me ever again, for your beauty will only cause me indefinite pain.

I am a man of my word, and therefore nothing you do may change the course of the path which I have chosen.

I apologise for misleading you, and I truly wish you the best. Thank you for every moment of joy you have brought me.

Yours sincerely,

Clarence D. Williams

Not bad, if she did say so herself. Now Autumn needed to work on the letter to Mr. Williams from Patience. Luckily, she and Autumn had similar handwriting, which would help a great deal in the process. That meant that she could also replicate her sister's signature... possibly. She'd better practice to be sure.

Autumn pulled out a crisp sheet of paper, dipped the feather pen in ink, and set to work. She wrote out 'Patience' in exotic cursive. Over and over again she wrote her sister's name, in her sister's hand.

"Swirls are all the rage these days," her sister had said when designing the *P* in her name.

"All those swirls drown out the letters!" Autumn had laughed.

"I know, but it's pretty."

Autumn smiled at the memory and stared at her practice signatures. Beautiful. She set to work and wrote the next letter.

Dear Sir,

I had every intention of addressing the concerns at hand in a more appropriate manner; however, I now find I am not able to bring myself to speak with you in the flesh.

Upon hours of consideration, of agonizing and regret, I realise I was rather hasty in accepting your proposal.

As you are aware, it is of utmost importance for women to venture out into society and find a man of grace, one who, above all, provides for his family through financial security. And while I comprehend your intentions are of great men with an unconditional desire to please, your greatest flaws are undoubtedly of the former.

In my sorrow I request to forfeit the matters of our engagement. I ask that you respect the choice I have made and refrain from any efforts to persuade me further from my settlements.

In order to hide my recent shame from society, I wish to cease all manner of association or greetings with you from this day forth, so not to spoil my reputation any further as a consequence of abandoning these past commitments.

I am truly embarrassed, even displeased, with my moral sense of accommodation, as I truly love you and hope you understand my reasoning for our separation. I have no grievances against you, nor your family, and wish you a successful and joyous career for your further days. Thank you for the gifts you have brought me and the entertaining stories you have told. I will never forget you.

Yours sincerely,

Patience Adriana Everleigh

Perfect. All Autumn needed now was to put the letters in envelopes and stamp one with Mr. Williams' seal. But getting Mr. Williams' seal would be a challenge. He always used a one-of-a-kind stamp in a shape particular to him. The worst part? He wore the stamp on a signet ring on his left index finger. Autumn couldn't just go and hold some hot wax up to his hand and ask him to press down for her! No, she would have to abandon her idea or find another way. Quitting wasn't an option; however, she herself didn't know how to forge a stamp. But come to think of it, she knew someone who might; a blind man by the name of Mr. Foster, who had once owned a printing shop and now worked for Mr. Glendale as an accountant. She knew this because she and her sister had once spent an early evening with Mr. Foster during a thunderstorm when they were forced to stay inside the Raven's Nest.

But what was she thinking? Of all the people she wanted help from, Mr. Foster was the last. After all, even if he could assist her in creating a stamp, which was highly unlikely given his physical condition, she didn't know him well enough to trust him in deciding her sister's fate! *But Patience needs me*, Autumn thought, deliberately not imagining her own life without Patience. She had to keep Patience safe, and if trusting Mr. Foster was her only hope, then his assistance might be worth the risk... maybe. She gazed out of the window once again.

5

That very evening, Autumn went back to the Raven's Nest. When she arrived in the upstairs hallway, outside an office door, she heard the sound of a typewriter clicking away within.

She knocked and sucked in her breath, steeling herself.

A man inside cleared his throat. "Come in."

She turned the knob and pushed. The door screeched, begging to be put still as the hinges ground against one another.

"Mr. Foster?" Autumn's voice cracked in a high-pitched squeak as she stepped in. Cool air blew through the open window.

Mr. Foster faced her direction but, since he was blind, he seemed to be looking just to the left of where she stood. "Ah, you came just at the right moment!" he said, turning in his chair to face the window once again.

"Did I?" she asked, surprised by his extremely friendly, almost disrespectful, manner.

"Indeed. I have been trying to describe the essence of the sun all afternoon."

Autumn gave a small smile. Mr. Foster fancied writing but always had a hard time describing his settings as he couldn't see, poor soul. On the rare occasions they encountered each other, he invariably asked her questions about what things looked like. Autumn liked that side of him. He possessed a sort of innocence that she didn't see in anyone else but her own sister.

"The sun is like a person," she replied now. "The kind of person you adore more than life itself. They are your closest companion, your greatest pleasure, and your strongest ally. Not a star outshines them for they are the brightest. Not a soul outlives them for they live the longest. And not a soul outloves them for they are perfect; unique and colourful, bathing all they touch in rays of goodness."

Mr. Foster snapped his finger and turned back to the desk, "Much appreciated. Good evening, Miss Everleigh."

Autumn sighed, silently. "But, sir, I came here to speak with you."

Turning back to Autumn, he cocked his head, brows furrowing. "Forgive me. Caught up in my imagination once again. Tell me, how might I serve you tonight, Miss Everleigh?"

She shifted her weight to one foot as she stood in the doorway. "I have but one question, if you do not mind me taking up your time."

"I have nowhere else to be. Please, do sit."

"I appreciate your hospitality." Autumn took care to close the door softly and sat in a chair with wooden arms and a cushion embroidered with sunflowers. Books were spread out all over the room, on cluttered shelves and in open drawers labeled with three-dimensional titles like *Ink* and *Letters*. The thick desk before the man had just enough room for an oil lamp, a tray of scones, papers, and—by far the most interesting piece in the entire collection—a typewriter modified with tiny metal shapes glued to every key, each different in design.

Mr. Foster kicked back in his seat and lifted a cup from his saucer. "Tea?"

"Tea would be most welcome." She took the spare cup on the table and poured in the hot water with shaky hands, hoping not to spill anything on the important papers.

"Sugar?" He held up a small jar.

Autumn accepted the container, scooped the crystals into her cup, and stirred. "Now, if I may, Mr. Foster, you used to work at a printing press before you became an accountant, correct?"

He nodded.

"Wonderful! As it happens, I am currently in need of a stamp. A stamp for scaling letters." She took a sip of the steaming beverage. "Have you any knowledge of forging an exact copy of an existing stamp?"

"Do you have the model you want to recreate?"

"Well, no. Not exactly, that is. I could perhaps obtain a piece of wax bearing the imprint of the design." Autumn had no idea how she would get this wax she spoke of but expected Mr. Williams might have some old seals with his crest lying around at Perlyn Hall.

"That should do, then I would simply reverse engineer it. The other option would be to sculpt a new stamp, but it wouldn't be identical to the original."

"You could do that?"

"Were you expecting someone else?"

"Oh, no, no. I am sure you are very capable but—" She stopped, struggling to find words.

Mr. Foster opened a drawer and produced a stamp. "This is my personal seal. I created it myself. *After* I lost my sight."

She swallowed, not able to deny the complexity of the craftsmanship. However, she had much hoped that he would tell her how to make one on her own, not offer to do it himself! His blindness was clearly no barrier but he was forgetful, his head forever stuck in the clouds. For all she knew, he would take weeks or more to give her something half worth using! Even if he created a perfect replica, it would be too late, and Patience would be married, and all would be lost. No, she couldn't let this man decide her and her sister's fate.

"Mr. Foster, I am afraid that I cannot accept." She stood and stepped to the door, then tightened her fingers on the knob and froze.

Autumn needed the stamp. She couldn't let Patience fall to destruction. But nor could she trust Mr. Foster. Unless... perhaps if she made sure to pay close attention that he did the job right and on time, she would minimise the risk of failure. Yes, she had to, even if she didn't like it.

"Mr. Foster, I... I have changed my mind. Name your price, if you would be so kind?"

He rotated in his chair so he faced the window, light from the setting sun cascading over his face in pink pigments, highlighting a thin, almost invisible line of soft facial hair. He sat still, blinking, not saying a word. Just gazing, unseeingly, into the horizon.

Autumn tapped her foot on the carpet. "I would pay you fairly."

Still no answer. Had he fallen asleep? She put her hands together and clapped twice. That ought to wake him up.

"Here's what I will do," he said at last. "I will create this stamp for you if you help me in return." Mr. Foster turned towards Autumn once more. "As you have probably put together by now, aside from being an accountant, I am also a writer. It is my most cherished hobby, which I hope to one day turn into a successful career. Despite my attempts in the craft, I am yet to find success. I am writing an article, and my future image depends on getting it perfect. I have only a few weeks left to finish the edit—"

"Oh, n-no." Wasn't it enough that she was trusting him as it was?

"Please, consider it. I don't need much. An hour or so of your time at most."

Autumn shook her head, "I will pay you double the amount you would usually charge."

"You need me, and I need your writing skills."

"But, sir, I don't have any writing skills! I have no real experience!" She tugged at her necklace so the beads dug into her neck. "Surely there is someone more talented than I."

"I am sure there is. But tell me, who else may I reach within a timely manner? I have but one chance to make this work, and you are the solution."

"A day then. I can help you for one day. You may accompany me on business terms on my trip to Perlyn Hall tomorrow and use my skills along the way. When we get back, you will make the stamp under my watch, and we will both go on our own separate ways. My hand is out, if you wish to shake it." She leaned forward, balancing her stomach on the desk and giving an unavoidable grunt from the pressure.

He reached his hand in the wrong direction and moved his arm until he smacked her fingers quite hard.

"Ow!"

"I apologise."

"Half a day." She squeezed her sore hand. "Half a day, and then you make my stamp."

"Deal."

She extended her hand and touched his at a slow pace, and they shook.

"Miss Everleigh, one more thing. Will you promise not to tell anyone that you assisted me with my writing? It is important that I do not... that is, that I..."

"Of course. In turn you must promise not to tell a soul about the stamp."

"Done. Tomorrow."

"Eight o'clock."

Autumn tied the black ribbon on her parcel, sealing the freshly baked pumpkin loaf with a cloth, then placed it in her handbag. She needed the food as an excuse for calling on Mr. Williams. The bread would be regarded as a sort of peace offering, to help lower the suspicion of her interference after she posted the letters. Of course, she wouldn't have any letters to post if she didn't find a wax seal at Perlyn Hall today.

Autumn glanced out of her kitchen window; outside didn't look pleasing at all. Winter wasn't far around the corner. Even the plants shivered from the morning frost across the ground.

She went upstairs to collect her thin gloves and her bag.

Nasty boots! Autumn yanked on the leather. *A small child could hardly fit these without crying.*

"Arr!" She did her best not to wake her sleeping sister.

Autumn got her first foot halfway in and managed to cram in the second a little. She stood, wobbling.

She squeezed her fists together and slammed all her weight into the walking boots.

"Ooh..."

Patience stirred in the bed.

Autumn held her breath as she bent down to button up her shoes, weaving the buttonhook in and out of the holes.

She would never get the tight footwear off tonight. Oh well, at least she was nearly ready. Handbag. Boots. Fan? She hurried over to the dresser. There were two drawers, one for her and one for her sister. She opened hers and pulled out the random baubles within. Perfume, hairpins... Oh, she had better not be late! Mr. Foster may start without her, which wouldn't necessarily be a terrible thing, but she had promised to help him, and she could never go back on a promise she had made.

Ah, there! She spotted the fan peeping out from under a stocking.

She finished by setting a grey chiffon cape over her shoulders. She wore her white, elbow-length gloves and purple visiting dress with lace ruffles. On her head was a simple bonnet decorated in grey ribbon. Perfect.

She hoped the eggs she left for her sister would still be warm when she woke. She decided to leave a quick note in case Patience walked past the table.

Autumn found a nearby scrap of paper.

Patience, breakfast is waiting on the stove. Love, Autumn.

She pasted the message on the front door and left.

Brrr. She rubbed her arms in hopes of holding on to the last sliver of warmth from inside. The sun had better warm the air up soon. If she ignored the cold, Autumn had to admit the day looked beautiful. She put her hands behind her back and held onto her handbag as she walked with light steps, smiling as she entered the little copse between her house and the Raven's Nest. One could walk through the path in but a few minutes, yet there was still a sense of a real forest here; the trees were close together and old. Standing in the middle, one could see nothing but flora.

Autumn stopped to breathe in the lush scents of the season. Close to the path, the birds danced in the water of a tiny stream. Some nights, an owl called out from the branches of an oak tree. Almost all the leaves were dead now, blanketing the damp grass. But the occasional orange leaf still dangled from a branch as the wind tugged and pulled at the stem. Was Autumn so fond of this season because of her name? Perhaps it was that. *Or the sunsets*, she thought.

A crisp fog greeted her when she arrived at the Raven's Nest, covering the ground and creeping toward the front porch.

Autumn stepped back and shaded her eyes with her hand to gaze up.

The rooms within were alive and well, with maids hustling about preparing Saturday morning breakfast and doing various chores.

"Get up, master Francis," someone said from the second floor. "Your teeth aren't going to brush themselves."

A pair of arms held a tapestry out a window and started to beat it so that dust sifted through the air.

The front door opened, and Autumn flinched, dropping her bag on her foot. "Oh!"

"What's that?" Mr. Foster descended the steps, his hair jostling as he walked.

"Good morning, Mr. Foster." Autumn bent down and clasped her bag, snapping upright and wiping off the sides. "Ridiculous," she mumbled so he wouldn't hear.

Mr. Foster carried a walking stick under his arm that morning and wore winter gloves and a thick, ankle-length overcoat. A leather satchel hung at his side. "It's quite a wonderful morning, isn't it? Crisp air. Good for the bones."

Autumn glanced around at the trees and frost. "Yes, it really is."

Mr. Foster pulled out his stick, tossed it into the air, caught it, and then tapped the tip over the ground.

Autumn put her hands against her face and puffed up her cheeks, setting out toward town with Mr. Foster trailing behind. She kept glancing over her shoulder to make sure he hadn't gotten himself lost. He was there every time, walking along and tapping the tip of his cane with his left hand.

They soon arrived in Carlisle to find a collection of carriages rolling through the steamy cobblestone streets, carrying elegant men and women all dressed for the weather, the men in coats and gloves and the women in thick furs.

"Stay close," said Autumn, "I don't want you getting lost in this crowd."

"I never get lost," said Mr. Foster, and to her horror, he tucked his cane under his arm and braved the chaos of the streets without any guidance whatsoever.

"Do be more careful!" She winced, sure he would collide with an oncoming traveller or horse. Thankfully, he did neither.

A train whistled in the nearby station, causing Autumn's insides to twist.

"A train ride would be nice at this hour..." said Mr. Foster, and he jingled some coins in his pocket.

"Inconceivable!"

"But it's warm."

"And we could die!"

"We would not die."

"It is not your place to decide."

The looming pillars of the station overlooked the road as fog breathed from within, bubbling into the murky streets and dousing her lower skirts in moisture.

Autumn squeezed her arms against her chest with fists facing up and stepped into the gaping shadows of the elegant structure.

"All aboard! Last call for the Ainlen and Port express!" cried a man in a fancy suit as he wound his fingers around the chain of his pocket watch. "Last call!"

"Goodness." Autumn shuddered. She wouldn't be caught dead on a train. Why, she would much rather ride a horse, which would be almost as frightening!

She and Mr. Foster left the station and continued down the next street, where all the nice big stores were, some four stories high and with slanted or domed roofs. Here the streets were wider, offering room for more people and dozens of lampposts, all put out.

Autumn seldom came this way as she couldn't afford the luxury of new clothing. Still, she couldn't help peeking in some of the windows now as they passed. So many displays and signs. Suits, dresses, shoes, and furniture—items she could never afford so long as she saved for a house.

Jewellery lined the next display, and Autumn put her nose near the glass, cupping her hands around the sides of her eyes to admire a golden bracelet.

She didn't own many ornaments like this one herself, aside from her necklace with the ring and another band on her right hand that her sister had made for her.

The golden bracelet in the display suggested an old shell, simplistic yet intricate in design. If a bracelet could embody a person, this one captured Patience boiled down to her essence. Pure and detailed, sunny and bright, so full of life. The last time Autumn walked around town had been with her sister close at hand.

"They've got in a new shipment of books!" Patience had pulled Autumn toward a display.

"Oh, Patty, how wonderful!"

"I will buy them all and read to you every evening!"

Autumn pulled at the tips of her left-hand fingers, starting with the thumb and working her way to the pinky.

Those happy times were long gone. If only Patience would love her as she once had.

"Paper! Get your morning paper right here!" A boy on the pavement waved a smudgy black bundle with one hand and wiped his grimy face with the other. "Lifeboat *Eliza Adams* lost at sea! Eleven men dead! Read all about it!"

"Ah." Mr. Foster dug a fist into his pocket. "I'll take one, please." He produced a few coins. "Miss Everleigh, would you kindly...?"

Autumn withdrew from the thoughts of her sister and took the money from Mr. Foster. Her face flickered back in the clouded reflection before she dropped the coins into the child's shaky fingers. The boy handed her the paper in return.

"Honestly, what do you need that paper for?" she hissed when they were well away from the boy.

Mr. Foster lowered his tone, "It's not that I needed the paper but rather that he needed the money."

"Ah, but now you're out a few pence."

He shrugged. "I try to help those fellows out as much I can. They are in a rather hard place."

Autumn's heart throbbed. Yes, she knew all too well what it was like to go hungry some days, without a halfpenny to spare.

She pulled back the front page of the paper as they continued on, her fingers tightening as she read, "*World Traveller Clarence Williams Finds a Wife!*"

Autumn glanced over the article, catching the use of her sister's name multiple times. Honestly! That man was exploiting his personal life and Patience's for publicity. His downfall would come, and he would soon be sorry.

"Mr. Foster, would you mind if I were to purchase this paper from you?"

"Oh, but I had hoped to read it...! No, of course you may. Never mind paying me."

"Why, thank you." Autumn stuffed the paper in her bag, smiling.

"Although I must ask," he said and tapped his stick against the cobblestone with two clicks. "They should be here about now. Or are they over there?" He grumbled something under his breath she couldn't hear. "No matter! Do you see a carriage and a few horses sitting about?"

"Whatever do you suggest?"

"I arranged a carriage for us yesterday."

Autumn planted both feet into the ground, and Mr. Foster bumped into her. "I should have known walking wasn't good enough for you. First the train and now this?"

Mr. Foster felt his nose, which had collided with her head, and squinted. "But—"

"I simply refuse to ride a carriage. Of all the vulgar suggestions!" She spun around and took off, making her steps as long as she could despite her constraining dress, the wind lashing at her face and stinging her skin.

"You don't enjoy them?" He paced after her.

"Not in the slightest! They are far too dangerous! I can barely tolerate the excursion once a year when I take my sister to see a performance of *A Christmas Carol*. I much prefer to run, for I like the wind. Although I usually walk, so as not to risk falling."

"I assure you it's perfectly safe. I've been in many carriages before."

"Well, jolly good for you!" Her cheeks and the tip of her nose were growing pink from the cold, so she put her gloves to her face again, rubbing them in circles.

They strode on until they had left Carlisle and entered the winding paths of the countryside. Fewer travellers were on the paths, leaving them to walk in the presence of chirping birds.

"And now," Mr. Foster deepened his voice, "the weary travellers stumble on their way, parched, in need of shelter, and with nothing but a few bread crumbs to their name... They begin to question whether they will live or die..."

Autumn shook her head; she couldn't help but smile a little.

"So," said Mr. Foster and snapped his finger three times. "I suppose we can improve on my writing, if you so desire." He tucked his stick behind the strap of the satchel at his back. "I brought some of my work for you to look over." He flipped open the leather satchel and took out a package, revealing some sort of treat. "Are you hungry?"

"Oh, no, no. You eat it."

He popped a piece of the food in his mouth.

She squeezed her stomach so he wouldn't hear the grumbling. Perhaps she should try some; he had offered after all. "May I be as uncivil as to inquire the attributes of the sustenance you present?"

He smacked his lips and wiped the spare crumbs off his chin. "Peanut brittle. Smoothest texture in all of Carlisle. Salty. Delicious."

Autumn slapped a hand against her upper chest and felt a sharp pain as she pushed her ring into her skin. "Oh, how... that sounds..."

"I fear you may regret your refusal. It is perfectly delicious."

"I am honoured by your kindness, but no, thank you! Honestly!" She eyed the ground, her face growing hot. "Sorry."

"You needn't worry," he said lightly. He cleared his throat and extended a paper toward her. "This is a section of the writing I am working on. You can read this over, and we can go on from there."

She slowed her pace as she read. The text elaborated on some of the descriptions she had given him before.

"Fine, fine." She tapped her teeth together and touched the paper against his fingers for him to take. He accepted it and dug around in his bag.

Autumn smoothed her hands over her hair, which was pinned firmly in a bun to withstand the breeze. Mr. Foster must indeed be desperate to want her help.

"Here is another piece."

She took the papers, which were upside down.

"Let me see..." She tilted her head around while rotating the papers. "What do you mean by describing dancing as 'a stuffy pastime of which humans partake, in the hopes of making a fragile connection'? And 'full of tiresome, repetitive moves'...? Goodness me!"

Mr. Foster ran his fingers up and down the strap of his bag and coloured slightly. "Not... descriptive enough?"

Autumn giggled. "No, not even close! Dancing is not merely an exercise we do to be polite or with hopes of winning someone's affection. Rather, dancing is the most wonderful and extraordinary feeling in the whole entire world! It's when you fall into the arms of someone you adore and admire and completely lose yourself in a trance. Time stops, and it's just you and your father swaying back and forth, forever more." She clutched the papers to her chest.

"It's bliss," she added and closed her eyes.

"Yes. I suppose that could work."

Autumn's eyes shot open, and she let her jaw drop. "I don't know who you have danced with, but—"

"Well, that's just it." He scratched the back of his neck, his tone sullen. "I haven't danced in rather a long time..."

"Oh." Well, that explained a lot about his description. "You really aren't missing much. Dancing is quite a wretched ritual. Quite boring."

"I thought you said dancing was the most wonderful and extraordinary feeling in the whole entire world?"

"Well, it's not! Not really. Hasn't been since—" she clasped her hand over her mouth. She suddenly felt that she might cry.

"Pardon?"

"It's none of your business," Autumn wiped her eyes, her voice growing thick. "If I desired to continue, then I would have."

Both grew very quiet, and Autumn didn't speak for some time. They walked in silence until Autumn felt stronger. She began commenting on his work once more.

"I appreciate all the information you have given me," said Mr. Foster as they neared Perlyn Hall. They walked amid fields and the occasional tree now.

"I am a woman of my word."

"We can finish the rest on our way back."

"You have more?"

"Yes. If it's too much for you, we can always sort through the other writings tomorrow."

"Goodness, no! We shall finish today. You'll just have to wait until I'm done with my business with Mr. Williams. I'll try to be quick. God knows I shan't want to stay long, anyhow."

They rounded a corner, coming upon the massive black gates of Perlyn Hall.

"Goodness," Autumn lost her breath. Such a home would never cease to amaze her. Adorning the tall gates were many swirls and gold details of various intricate designs depicting lions, boars, birds and other creatures. Beyond the entrance, the path crept upward toward the pool, which reflected generous amounts of sunlight on the rippling water. The centrepiece, of course, was the home itself, which was five times the size of the Raven's Nest and built in a perfect rectangle of beige stone.

The roof was flat and displayed several small towers, including the crown jewel of them all: an observatory topped with a green dome, designed for stargazing.

Autumn clutched her stomach as they climbed the marble steps to the door with an archway above.

This was it. Her last   her only—chance to save her sister.

6

Mr. Foster sat in an armchair in the drawing room of Perlyn Hall, tapping his foot against the carpet and sipping the tea the maid had provided for him. "Not bad. Could use a hint of sugar, though," he commented.

Autumn propped her head up with her hands and gazed around the room. It was richly decorated with draperies, footstools, clocks, tables and, most interestingly, ornate birdcages.

She sighed. If she stayed still any longer, she would melt into a puddle.

Autumn flipped open her white-satin fan and cooled her warm cheeks, letting her lips sag as she unloaded as much air from her diaphragm as she could without passing out.

She snapped the fan shut against her palm abruptly. She shouldn't have to wait here any longer.

She had two options: stay here and wait for Mr. Williams, somehow come up with an excuse to search his home for a wax seal and then liberate that wax seal from his home, or leave now. Empty handed. While the latter would not provide the outcome she desired, it would mean there was no danger of being caught snooping through someone's things.

But she wouldn't get caught. No. For if anyone found her, she would say she had lost her way while admiring the decor! Wonderful. A third option presented itself to Autumn. The heat in the room made up her mind for her.

"I shall return to you presently," Autumn stood and brushed out the wrinkles in her dress with one hand.

"What? Wherever are you going?"

"My complexion is in desperate need of... a change of temperature."

"You know, you shouldn't go poking around in other people's homes without their permission."

Autumn laughed lightly, as if the very idea had ever occurred to her in her life and she thought the premise a great joke. "Oh, Mr. Foster! You devil! I don't see any problem with stretching my muscles and cooling down a little. Besides, the servants said we had the place to ourselves, didn't they?"

"I suppose..." He scratched his neck. He must have been rather warm too. She would have invited him to come explore with her, but he needed to stay behind in case Mr. Williams returned.

"I'll be but a minute, you shan't notice my absence before I return." She stuffed her fan in her bag and slid the strap over her wrist.

Mr. Foster crossed his arms and leaned far back into his seat. "And what do I do when Mr. Williams arrives and I am the only one here?"

Autumn touched her teeth together and shifted her focus to the door. "If Mr. Williams appears, then tell him that I have brought a gift and that you were accompanying me today on business, as that is the truth. And if he asks where I am, say that I'm stretching my legs as I'm terribly warm and... and will be back momentarily."

"Of course. Don't forget about me, now."

"Never." She crept toward the door and rested both hands on the glossy surface. She drew in her breath, filling her cheeks with air as she pushed the door open.

Autumn stuck her face into the vacant hall, ready to withdraw if someone came by. Empty. Good.

She crept out, taking tiny steps and peering from left to right while biting her lower lip.

Where should she go first? If Mr. Williams had any letters lying around with his crest on them, they would likely be in his study. Where was his study?

She pulled out her fan again and whipped it open. It was cooler in the hall and she found she could think more clearly. Yes, she remembered now, she had caught sight of such a room during a previous visit, when Mr. Williams showed them the dining hall, the grand entry and the ballroom. They had also passed a room with a large desk in the middle; that was surely the study.

Autumn ventured down the hall, gently fanning her face as she went. She squinted but couldn't make out the end of the antechamber. The high ceilings judged her every move. She tightened her leg muscles as she walked and lowered her shoulders as she stepped into the shadows of the various collectibles from Mr. Williams' travels. Between each exhibit, a tall arched window let in the light, and she found herself passing in and out of pools of darkness.

An old suit of armour stole her attention. The knight stood tall, with one leg forward and both hands grasping his sword.

Autumn nodded to him, imagining what it would be like to start a conversation. They might compare their lives, and she would hear from him the challenges of fighting for his kingdom in the midst of a war. Would he ever make it home to his wife and children? They probably missed him. But how ridiculous!

Autumn moved on past the valuables and glorious baubles to stumble upon the first room. The walls within hugged a chair and rather dingy bathtub.

The next threshold led to a smaller hall producing a new series of doors. She approached the first and grasped the door handle. Her hand slipped from the knob as her stomach tightened, half expecting someone to jump out at her. The place, however, stood empty.

The room inside turned out to be a music room, full of floor-to-ceiling windows. In the far corner, a beautiful pianoforte welcomed her. It was glorious, despite the various cracks in the wooden surface. A shiny harp and several colourful chairs with rose designs were arranged on a carpet beneath the chandelier, which cast flickering rainbows across the many busts on pedestals lining the walls.

Autumn took care to close the door with a soft click as she stepped in. She noticed a small card table in one corner and upon further investigation, discovered several large boxes of cigars.

"How on earth do men smoke these things?" she shuddered. She had been told the fumes were rather ghastly to breathe in, and she always found herself choking when walking past a room of active pipes. It was a good thing, she thought, that it was intolerable for a gentleman to smoke in the presence of a woman, otherwise she would have to avoid men altogether.

Autumn wished she could stay now. She would sit in one of those beautiful chairs. A sonata in B minor would sound wonderful on the pianoforte; sadly, there was not the time.

She gave one last, longing glance at the room and left by way of another door, at the far end, which led to the dining hall. Ah yes, she had been here before and had the pleasure of eating at the table with a few other guests one fine evening. If only she had known then what Mr. Williams had in store for her and her sister. Autumn could have prevented all this drama early on.

"Good day, miss," said a plump woman when Autumn reentered the hall. "Can I help you with anything?"

Autumn turned to face the woman, who had a wide smile, pink cheeks, a mobcap, and a tray of pastries in her hands. Autumn eyed the sweets and inhaled. Berry. She could almost taste the strudel.

The woman nodded, waiting for Autumn to speak.

She could ask her where Mr. Williams kept his study. No, that would be too nosy. "Oh, do forgive me, I am just looking around at the treasures. I'm a guest of Mr. Williams."

The lady mumbled something before she curtsied and slipped away as quietly as she had arrived.

Autumn found the next room and took notice of how the door hadn't been properly closed all the way, so she stuck her nose in a little. A fire crackled away inside.

She let out her breath and entered. Shelves and shelves of leatherbound books... A library!

The shelves were packed with writings and went from floor to ceiling. A huge, rolling ladder waited; the room, and the shelves, were almost twice Autumn's height.

Autumn closed the door and hurried over to the ladder. She squeezed the rungs and took a step up, kicking off the ground and rolling a few inches. How jolly! She should bring Patience here sometime; they would have so much fun reading together! Oh, wait. They still weren't speaking. Autumn let go of the ladder and examined the space. A small desk at the corner of the room caught her attention. She headed over to investigate.

Stacks upon stacks of books lined the floor with at least a dozen or so open on the desk itself. Crinkled letters, a pair of gold-rimmed reading glasses and stray papers were among the great tomes. Nothing bore a wax seal, however.

Autumn leaned her head to the side as she walked around the desk, gazing over some of the open pages, all of which were novels: *Gulliver's Travels*, *The Adventures of Mr. Verdant Green*, *Robinson Crusoe*.

Autumn moved to the back of the desk to try her luck at some of the drawers.

She set her handbag down and pulled on one of the handles. The wood let out a piercing shriek, spreading goose bumps down her uncovered upper arms. Goodness! Autumn pulled her hands to her chest and shot a look at the door. No one else had heard. Thank goodness. The inside of the compartment looked much as a squeaky old drawer ought; old and tired, filled with dangling cobwebs, broken pencils, ink and an ancient handkerchief.

She fingered the handle of the next drawer and clenched her teeth together, bracing herself for the inevitable squeak. Sure enough, the drawer delivered, putting up quite the commotion. The closest thing Autumn could compare the sound to was that of rubbing a piece of metal along a schoolroom chalkboard as hard as one could. Master Francis certainly enjoyed doing that all too often to give the maids—and even herself—a good scare.

Autumn moved on to search the drawer, shoving the rummage aside and failing to see the bottom. She lifted out some papers and stacked them in a neat little pile on the carpet, handling them carefully so as not to tear or soil any in the process. Autumn pushed the big chair aside and lifted her skirts, seating herself on the floor. This could take a while, so she might as well make herself as comfortable as possible.

The papers within were rather boring. Just a collection of filthy newspapers covered with grime. Honestly, Mr. Williams should clean more often. She took out another paper, the words reading sideways. She turned it around and examined the title: *Clarence Williams Takes on France.*

She set it to the side and took out the next: *Clarence Williams Crosses the Pacific Ocean.*

He must think rather highly of himself, indeed, if he felt the need to keep all these old stories. Autumn went on to the next: *Clarence Williams Visits Spain.*

She began to arrange the papers beside one another on the floor, organizing them by date, starting with *Clarence Williams Leaves England to Seek Adventure* leading to the last with the headline *Clarence Williams Returns from Angola, Africa.*

She gasped, eyes darting across the collection of articles.

Autumn groped around for her bag, digging inside until she found the headline from earlier, *World Traveller Clarence Williams Finds A Wife!*, and set it at the end of the row of papers she had laid out on the rug.

"Oh, no." A shiver clutched her spine, her eyes welling with tears. "No, no, no..." She could barely breath.

Mr. Williams really didn't care about her sister after all. She was just a stepping stone, another headline in his life! Patience was a newspaper title, a title to be replaced like each of its predecessors, with the next inevitably being *Clarence Williams Embarks on World Tour.*

Autumn sniffled as she made a fist and covered her mouth, trying to stem the flow of tears. It wouldn't do to panic.

Mr. Williams was even worse than she had imagined. She should have seen it before. He was a success chaser, and Patience was merely another prize on his plate. Not only was he a dangerous man, one who wasted his fortune on travels, but he was also a self-centred one, a greedy one.

Patience didn't deserve this; she deserved to be treated as the centre of the world, not some temporary treasure to be tossed aside when something bigger came along.

At that moment, the library door was flung open and a light cry of surprise escaped Autumn's lips.

She froze, ceasing her breath. She had done it now. She would be discovered. Discovered just like this, on the floor with papers in her hands, papers that most certainly did not belong to her. Oh, she should never have come here. She should have stayed home; she should have tried again to reason with—

Boot heels clicked across the room. Autumn shivered.

The steps ceased.

She closed her eyes. This was the end. She could never explain herself now.

Still, more silence.

Autumn wrapped her shaky fingers around a leg of the desk and leaned froward to take a peek.

Someone stood across from her, facing a nearby shelf. She tried to get a better look, but a large bookcase blocked most of the figure. The person gave no indication they had seen Autumn. She watched with wide eyes, waiting to be discovered at any moment.

The person reached up to a shelf, took down a book with a yellow cover and sneezed. Autumn flinched, smacking her hand against the wooden desk. She winced and pulled her hand close. She held her breath.

The footsteps tapped away. The door slammed shut. They were gone.

Autumn held her throbbing hand to her chest and sighed her relief. She was safe. She hadn't been discovered. Thank goodness! She fought the absurd urge to giggle. *Get out of here before someone else comes along!*

With shaky fingers, Autumn collected the front page of each of the newspapers and folded the pages carefully into her bag. She would show them to Patience when she arrived home tonight. Once her sister saw this, she could not deny that Mr. Williams was a scoundrel. But Autumn still needed that seal. Just in case.

So now what? She bit her lip as she once more stood in the empty hall, eyes puffy from her tears. She couldn't return empty handed; she needed the wax imprint of Mr. Williams' crest.

There was a room across from her; she might as well look. She walked over and pushed the door. Nothing. She pushed again, but the door was locked.

Autumn rested her head on the door and let her hand slide down the wood. Her fingers collided with something hard and cold. She twisted her fingers along the peculiar shape. Not the knob. No, far too small, much more like...

"A key!" She gave a small bounce of the shoulders and unlocked the door. She entered to find a massive brick fireplace flickering with life. Two large bookcases cluttered with various items rested on either side of a window near a desk with various objects sprawled across the top: a compass, an open sketch pad with an illustration of a gorilla, a magnifying glass and some small boxes labeled 'dirt samples' and 'native instruments.'

She inched her way into the room, ears red and heart still recovering from the scare in the library.

A massive world map on the wall caught Autumn's attention. This must be Mr. Williams' study. She squinted and cocked her head to the left as she examined the faded map with a red string connecting various locations together, starting with England and running down along the borders of France and Spain, then crossing the Atlantic Ocean to Africa, and then back to England. This must be everywhere Mr. Williams had travelled in his life.

Her gaze drifted to the two notes pinned on the map. One was titled *Percy's Adventures*, and proceeded to name a dozen or so countries and continents. The paper beside it read *worthless*, with nothing else printed.

Autumn left the map, went to the desk, and pulled out the first drawer. To her amazement, the wood didn't squeak at all! The inside of the compartment featured a notepad with pen and ink. She moved on to the next and removed a stack of papers. A flash of red captured her attention. She reached down with trembling hands and clasped the letter, wrinkled and faded. A dab of dry wax sealing it in place had the image of a maple leaf covered in swirls: Mr. Williams' seal.

Autumn ran her fingers along the textures of the wax, closing her eyes. "Thank you, Lord…"

Autumn's heart soared before she remembered she had no one with which to share her victory. She missed Patience. Missed her dearly. If only she didn't have to do all of this to protect her. For just a second she thought how wonderful it would be if Mr. Williams really was a good person, more dependable than herself. If that were the case, maybe she really could let Patience marry him. His home was so beautiful and Autumn knew Patience would love—

The study room door opened.

"Oh!" Autumn hurriedly stuffed the envelope into her purse.

Patience entered the room. "Mr. Williams—" She looked up, pupils expanding.

Autumn's heart skipped a beat as her stomach dropped.

"Autumn? What on earth are you doing here?"

"Me? Wh-what are *you* doing here?" She shoved the drawer shut and swallowed.

Patience's cheeks ignited with pink as she rubbed the side of her arm. "Mr. Williams and I were going to have a picnic. In the garden." She looked away.

"Oh. I see." Autumn's eyes drifted to the yellow book in Patience's gloved hands. So she had been the one in the library earlier!

"What happened to your face? Have you been crying?" Her sister pointed and raised her eyebrows.

Autumn wiped her eyes with her arm. "No, it's just all the dust in here." Which was partially true, as she felt there was a good deal of dust on her face from poking around in the drawers; Mr. Williams ought to have someone clean them more often.

"Here." Patience let out a puff of air and separated a small envelope from the book in her hand, thrusting it toward her sister while keeping her head down.

Autumn pulled off a glove, put her fingers in the corners of her eyes, and dabbed at the tears. "What's this?" She stepped out from behind the desk and accepted the letter, darting her eyes between it and her sister.

When Patience didn't answer, Autumn ripped open the flap and peered in. "Patience, what is this?"

"It's the money I owe you.

"What money?" Autumn knew very well what money.

"The savings I burned. I am replacing all I cost you. There's even some extra in there to make up for... my faults."

"Let me guess—you prompted Mr. Williams to fund this?"

"Well... yes."

Autumn thrust the envelope at her sister. "Take it." As much as she wanted the money, she couldn't let Patience win. Not when she still hadn't apologised for what she had done. This didn't make up for any-thing.

"It's a gift," Patience insisted.

"I don't want it."

"If you don't take it, it will all go to waste."

"Fine. Someone else can enjoy it." Autumn tossed the envelope at the floor.

"Must you be so inconsiderate?" Patience stamped her foot and scrunched up her face. Of course, her features were too soft to be truly menacing. She resembled an inconvenienced child.

Patience continued, "I am being sincere for once and trying to make things right, and you only—"

"Make things right? How in the world does this fix anything between us? You haven't changed your mind about the marriage or how you feel, and yet you persist in tempting me to make yourself feel better about... about your sins!"

"My sins!"

"Miss Patience, are you in here?" Mr. Williams appeared in the doorway. His face was lit with a smile.

The sisters shot him an icy glare. Autumn realised that they must have been quite the picture, her face blotchy and her eyes teary, Patience with narrowed eyes and flaming cheeks.

Mr. Williams' face sank. "Did I interrupt something?"

"No," the sisters said in unison. They locked eyes and frowned at one another.

"Miss Everleigh, I am surprised to see you here. You are most welcome, as always, of course—"

Patience crossed her arms, confusion twisting her brows. "I am surprised, as well. What were you doing alone in Mr. Williams' study?"

Autumn put her glove back on and busied herself with her handbag while her mind raced.

The bread!

She slid her bag off of her wrist. "I- I know I am without a calling card, and I hope you will forgive me, but... but I... I brought you a gift," She extended the loaf to Mr. Williams.

"Well, now look who's trying to make herself feel better," Patience stamped her foot.

Autumn ignored her sister and unwrapped the bread. "A pumpkin loaf!" she announced. Her smile was tight.

Mr. Williams accepted the package and eyed the ceiling. "Miss Everleigh, would you do the honour of joining us on our picnic? It is the least I can offer."

A picnic sounded like a terrible idea. Any other day she would have loved it, but not today. Not when she disagreed with everyone at the meal. Yet, she might as well say yes. If the letters were going to look truly authentic, she would have to seem happy with the union.

"Yes, sir. I shall join you, thank you ever so much. Although you must know that Mr. Foster has accompanied me on my visit today and waits in the drawing room."

"I shall invite him as well." He opened the door wide. "After you, my dear."

Patience stooped down and picked up the envelope with the money, shooting her sister a glare as she left the room.

7

Autumn found that Mrs. Glendale was also visiting for the day. After a picnic lunch in the garden, Mr. Williams invited the party to take a leisurely stroll around the well-kept landscape of Perlyn Hall.

Autumn had eaten only a little of her meal, despite her gnawing hunger, as she was yet to recover from the shock of seeing her sister. She kept quiet, only speaking when spoken to. She noticed the same in Patience, who seldom went this long without chattering and asking questions. Any other day she would have been skipping around in circles, smacking people on the arms and speaking out of turn.

Throughout the late afternoon, any time Autumn and Patience locked eyes with one another, her body shook as she blew quick gusts of air through her nose. Everyone must have sensed the awkwardness between the women, but no one said a word about it.

Autumn longed to tell her sister about the newspapers. Patience would run to her with open arms and cry,

"Oh, Autty, the foolish girl that I am! I should have listened to you all along!"

And Autumn would comfort her with a gentle, "There, there, Pay-pay. Some tea will cheer you up now, darling. Let's go home."

Now, they all wandered through a path in the middle of one of the many gardens of Perlyn Hall.

The grounds behind the hall offered various trails, weaving in and out of trees and around ponds. Flower beds featured different shades of purples and pinks and tucked away in one area was an elegant, cone-shaped gazebo where one could sit and enjoy tea without the disturbance of others.

As they strolled away from the building, the path led them to a stone bridge that crossed a brook and brought them to a lake where the sun cast a pinkish glow over the waters, delighting the croaking frogs and whispering fish. A small island sat in the middle of the lake, exploding with well-tended chrysanthemums.

My, how lovely it would be to live here all your life, Autumn thought. To watch the plants blossom in the spring, swim in the lovely lake in summer, stroll the property by fall, and sit inside near the fireplace snug with tea come wintertime.

"May I direct your attention to these figures?" said Mr. Williams as they walked the shaded path around lake. He pointed to a fine marble statue of a couple, the man handing the female figure his heart. "This one happens to be my personal favourite."

Autumn sensed that even Mr. Williams was not his normal self while in her presence. He must feel awkward for being at odds with her. And rightly so.

Mr. Foster reached his hand forward, moving his fingers along the faces of the statues. "Such fine detail."

"Yes." Mr. Williams stroked his mustache, Adam's apple quivering. "They reflect the story of a king whose love is tested a thousand times over. Every challenge he faces brings him destruction, but he pushes through, eventually losing all he possessed save for his heart, which he kept to maintain the cherished relationship with his caring wife." He shot a sideways glance at Autumn, ears red.

She made a tight smile, knowing he meant to make her feel better. But he couldn't, for he still had not changed his intentions any more than her sister had.

Mr. Williams wrung his hands and walked on to the next statue, followed by Patience and Mr. Foster.

Autumn hesitated, catching sight of Mrs. Glendale standing off to the side in the grass near the water. She had to admit that the setting sun and light breeze made the woman quite a sight to behold. Autumn had never noticed how truly beautiful she was until now, with her dark brown hair and slender figure. She seemed to be at peace in that moment.

"Oh, Mrs. Glendale." Autumn approached her to let her know the rest of the party had moved on. The woman didn't answer or even move as the breeze rustled her cape.

"Madam," Autumn said, moving closer. "Your brother has continued on down the path."

Mrs. Glendale blinked slowly and opened her mouth a crack. Her voice was a frail whisper. "Mother? Has Percy returned?"

Autumn cocked her head, eyebrows furrowing. "Not Percy, madam. Your brother, Clarence."

"Oh..." Mrs. Glendale folded her hands, tears streaming down her face as she faced Autumn. "And you are not my mother..."

"I am afraid I am not." She bit one side of her lip and reached out to take the lady's hands. "Mrs. Glendale, are you quite well?"

The woman blinked quickly. "Yes," she said, her voice wavering uncertainly. She lowered her head, her cheeks pink. "Yes, yes. Of course. Forgive me. I was lost in my drifting thoughts."

Autumn placed the woman's left hand on her arm and led her back to the path, wondering what on earth had happened to the poor lady. She had never spoken of her late mother before, let alone a Percy. Autumn longed to ask questions but refrained from speaking, not wanting to upset her.

They soon caught up with the group and, when they finished their stroll, they headed back indoors to enjoy some evening tea.

Autumn took a long sip of her drink, admiring the blue tapestries on the golden walls.

Mr. Williams cleared his throat. "Miss Everleigh, would it be within your interest to be entertained in the atmosphere of my astronomy tower once we finish our tea this evening?"

"If you so desire."

Patience set her cup down on her saucer. "I have always wanted to look through a telescope. This will be most pleasant."

The wooden doors of the room creaked open, revealing a servant who bowed. "Mr. Williams. A man by the name of Gregory Winston is here on behalf of the press and wishes to speak with you regarding your upcoming travels."

Mr. Williams stood rather briskly, wiping his face with a handkerchief. "Tell him I am home."

The servant went on his way.

"I suppose this is where we part ways," Mr. Williams sighed. He wrung his hands and faced the company.

"Thank you for having us," said Autumn. "You have a most charming house."

"Must Miss Patience leave us so soon?" Mrs. Glendale asked, eyes tired. "I had so hoped to show her some of the books in the library. Maybe you could stay for supper?"

Patience put a finger under her lower lip and faced Autumn as if asking for permission.

"It is awfully late," said Autumn.

"Nonsense," said Mrs. Glendale. "She may spend the night here, then."

Autumn opened her mouth and shut it, fire igniting inside. Mrs. Glendale was trying to keep her and Patience apart!

"Miss Everleigh, might I have the privilege of seeing you out?" Mr. Williams said, pulling out his pocket watch and giving it a shake. "Blasted thing never works."

"I can manage perfectly well on my own, thank you."

"I insist." He headed for the door while eyeing the time. Mr. Foster followed close behind.

"Mrs. Glendale." Autumn lifted her dress a bit and bent her knees in a curtsy. "I love you," she whispered to Patience, who said nothing in return and only stared with saddened eyes.

Autumn left, weeping a little as she followed her host to the front door.

"I hope you had a pleasant visit," Mr. Williams said to Autumn as the three stood on the front porch, the sun nearly set and the orange light from the lamp burning above them.

"As well as I was able, despite our circumstances."

He stared at her, lips quivering as if he wanted to apologise. "Shall I arrange a carriage for you?"

"No, thank you." They focused on each other's faces, Autumn swallowing within her stinging throat.

Mr. Williams pulled his lips inward, making a tight smile. "You, um, may call upon me whenever you so desire. Name the day, and we will have another picnic. In your honour."

"Of course. Good evening." And she turned, heading down the front steps two at a time, holding her skirts so as not to trip, with Mr. Foster tapping his stick behind her. The front door closed with a heavy thud. Autumn shuddered, tears bleeding down her neck. She curled her fingers inward and raised them to her head, bending over so that loose tendrils of her hair flipped across her face.

She trembled as she cried, her breathing rapid. She felt perfectly distraught. Looking at Patience made her want to crumple on the floor. Her sister wasn't a wicked person at all, but rather kind and full of goodness. Earlier she looked like she wanted to cry just as much as Autumn herself did. If both sisters were suffering from this fighting, they couldn't go on like this. Their relationship was growing weaker by the minute. But yet, Patience was so stubborn. Autumn knew she would not give in.

Autumn stood over the dark pool in the front lawn and her teary reflection stared back at her. She needed to make up with her sister, for both their sakes. She had to post the letters.

8

October 21, 1866

Dear Diary,

Men wearing suits and eyeglasses came and knocked on our door. They told us to collect our things and go.

Life changed faster than any of us could comprehend.

With no other options, my mother, sister, and I were forced into one of the many workhouses across England. I had heard stories of widows and daughters without proper care having to go there, but I never thought I would be one of them. At twelve and six years old, Patience and I were expected to work alongside hundreds of other young women and children without a farthing to their name.

Days were long. Nights were hard. In return for our services, we earned two small, tasteless meals a day and a thin, mice-eaten bed for the three of us to share by night. We huddled together for warmth beneath ragged blankets as thin as paper without a single pillow.

Mama cried continuously and was punished when her tears interfered with her work. She soon learned to weep silently.

I did my best to spend my waking hours near my family but, despite my efforts, we were often separated. I sewed more clothes than I could count, spending all day bent over a table with needle and thread in hand. In and out went the needle, in and out, over and over again. I tried to pretend I was making embroideries at home, in the evening, but the process was far from relaxing.

I was forbidden from speaking with the other children, despite being one of several young girls crowded around the worktable. Poor Patience couldn't handle the stitching; to my horror, they took her away to be used as a chimney sweep. She always came back in tears, and whenever we were alone, I hugged her with all the love I could muster and whispered words of affection in her ear. And on a particularly rough day, I would open my lips to sing our special song.

"Hum ditty, hum ditty, off in a daydream,
Won't you come and dance with me?
Hum ditty, hum ditty, off in a daydream,
Won't you come and dance with me?"
Patience would always smile a little and join in,
"Hey oh, the whirlwind blows
Through the highs and through the lows.
Hey oh, the whirlwind blows
And sweeps us 'til the sun comes down."

These small moments of peace did little to make up for the loss of our past life, visiting the market, practicing the arts, and taking carriage trips to the countryside with Papa. And Mama's health took a bad turn.

"Eat." I would hold the porridge to her mouth, but she always refused my offer. She hadn't eaten a bite since we had entered the workhouse. If she went without sustenance much longer, she might perish.

"Please." I pushed the bowl into her hands. She shook her head no, eyes watery. I sighed, putting a hand on her shoulder. "We will be all right."

Later that evening, when all were asleep, I awoke to Mama stirring beside me.

"Jesper," she whispered. "Come back..."

"It's okay, Mama." I rubbed my hand in circles on her back, surprised at how warm her body was against my skin. I followed the heat to her neck and forehead. "You are burning up."

She said nothing, only pulled the blankets further over her body as she shivered.

"I shall try and find some water." As I rose from the bed, I heard a rat scurrying away. I shuddered before proceeding through the eerie workhouse at great speed.

When I arrived back with some water, I found that my mother had stopped shaking.

"Mama?" I whispered, jostling her gently. "Mama, wake up." I pulled at her hands. She lay motionless, not a single breath coming from her mouth. I refused to give up, dragging back the covers and listening for a heartbeat. None came.

I got back into the bed and lay close to her, sobbing all night and praying that she would wake in the morning. She didn't, and Patience and I never recovered.

In the earlier days, I had missed my father, and now, I grieved mother. We were living the consequences of Papa's choices. Mama was dead because she didn't have a husband to provide for her anymore. This wasn't her fault. It wasn't Patience's fault and, as hard as I tried, I couldn't see how it could possibly be mine. This was Papa's fault. His and no one else's. His choices had brought pain, suffering and heartache to his wife and his children. He'd done this to us, and there was no one to blame but him. Papa was a liar. He had promised to be there for me, for us, and he wasn't. The one man I knew to always keep his promises had broken them.

A sickness continued to spread, and many of the children living in the workhouse died. I had to keep Patience alive, so I did the most logical thing I could think of: I started feeding her my portions of food and giving her more of the blanket at night. I resorted to eating whatever she didn't, learning to cherish the few scraps of the nasty porridge, for even a small drop of substance calmed my aching stomach.

One day, after five children had been proclaimed dead within little more than a week, I received a wrinkled letter from an old friend of my mother, by the name of Helen Enfield. In the letter, the woman offered to come and take Patience to stay with her for a few weeks, as an alternative to the workhouse.

I had never met Mrs. Enfield, and I didn't know if she planned to treat my sister with the care she needed. If I couldn't even trust my own father to keep us safe, how could I trust this strange lady? She probably wanted to make Patience work for her as her personal chimney sweep, or her maid, or she might put her in the attic and forget all about her! But then again, this was a friend of Mother's, and Mama had never let me down. Besides, if Patience didn't get some fresh air far away from this sickness, she might perish. I had to let her go, whether I liked it or not.

As she had promised, Mrs. Enfield showed up later the next week and left with Patience, assuring me she would take good care of her and bring her back within a month's time.

"Goodbye, Patty, my love," I gave her a last hug, eyes teary, as I went back to my workbench.

My days got a whole lot worse. I found it hard to eat, sew, and sleep without worrying about my sister. Poor Patience, all alone in a strange home with a woman neither of us knew. If only I had assurance that she was well tended to, with good food, fresh clothes, and a comfy bed as she deserved...

When at last Patience did arrive back to me by carriage early the next month, we greeted one another with many hugs, but weren't able to properly talk together until later that evening, in bed.

We had to keep our voices low so as not to disturb the many other sleepers, but that didn't keep me from asking Patience questions. Was Mrs. Enfield nice? Was her home comfortable? Was the food tasty? She nodded in the dark. And then she stopped.

"Autumn," she whispered to me.

"Yes, Patience?"

"Please don't make me go back there again."

"Why ever not? What did Mrs. Enfield do?"

"It's not her. It's... it's Mr. Enfield."

My eyes widened, my chest tightening.

"He—" Patience swallowed.

"He what?"

Patience rolled back the sleeve of her dress, revealing an angry red welt on her arm.

"From his belt," she whispered. The mark felt very hot under my fingers.

I immediately burst into tears, caring not who I awoke as I cried and hugged Patience tight. The picture of her being beaten blossoming in my mind, taking root in my memory.

This was all my fault. I had been a fool to let Patience out of my sight. I had relied on Papa, then Mrs. Enfield, and both had lied.

After I stopped crying and kept apologizing over and over, I stroked my sister's pretty blonde hair and whispered, "Goodnight, Patience."

"Goodnight, Autumn. I'm going to miss you," she yawned. She sounded very young.

"Why, you're not going anywhere, are you?" I asked, my heart beating faster.

Patience giggled, snuggling deeper into the bedding. "No."

"And I'm certainly not going anywhere, am I?"

"No silly, but I won't be seeing you for a few hours because I'll be asleep."

"Oh, Patty, but you'll be unconscious the whole time."

"But I'll still miss you for every one of those minutes."

I couldn't help squeezing her. "Well, then, I shall miss you too."

She yawned and closed her eyes. I couldn't help but smile at my precious sister. My father may have left us, and my mother had died, but I still had Patience, and the only way to keep her safe was to rely on the one person who would never let me down: me. I made a solemn vow then to protect her for the rest of my life. She was all I had, now.

9

Autumn awoke the next morning with a yawn, then dragged herself out of bed.

After filling the washbasin and cleaning herself with a washcloth, she dressed. She placed a lace shawl over her shoulders and tidied her hair. She shook it free of a simple knot and styled her hair in an updo made of two separate, braided buns, one near the top of the head and the other at the back near her neck, connected by a long braid. She craned her neck to see the results in the mirror. Usually, Patience checked her hair from the back.

Once she was ready for the day, Autumn went downstairs to prepare breakfast. When she entered the confining hallway leading to the kitchen, she was surprised to find Patience already home. She was leaning against the striped wallpaper with her head in her hands.

"Hello, Patience," she said, her voice echoing oddly in the hollow space. She hadn't called her sister one of her pet names in days and longed to say *Pay-pay* or *Patty* again.

Patience slowly raised her gaze, revealing her sullen face and tangled curls, as she blinked away tears and said, "Hello." She gave a sort of tight smile that fell the moment it rose.

"What's the matter?" Autumn asked, almost reaching forward to touch her sister's arm but managing to keep to herself.

"Nothing. I'm fine." Patience locked her puffed-up eyes on Autumn's and cupped her hands, dropping them to her waist.

Autumn bit her lip and sucked in as much air as she could in a single breath. Patience ought to apologise; after all, she was being selfish for letting this go on for so long. Then again, maybe saying sorry wasn't that simple. She probably felt just as stuck as Autumn did, not knowing what to do next, feeling hopeless.

"Why are you crying?" Autumn ventured with a cracked voice, pressing her arms vertical to her chest and resting her chin on her knuckles.

"Because, because of us—" Patience choked on the whispered words and motioned between them.

Maybe now was the time for Autumn to tell her of all she had discovered at Perlyn Hall. Her sister might change her mind then and there, and they could hug and make up. *How truly wonderful that would be!* Then she could forgo forging letters altogether and put an end to this dreadful nonsense.

"I have something to show you." Autumn pulled at the tip of her sleeve. She had to protect Patience, even if that meant hurting her feelings.

Patience said nothing and put one finger on her under lower lip.

"Come," Autumn found her bag and led her sister to the drawing room. She proceeded with deliberate, unhurried movements, opening her bag and unfolding the newspapers within, to arrange them on the tea table one by one, as she had done on the library floor the day before.

"What is this?" Patience tilted her head, her face aglow with curiosity.

Autumn dug her nails into her palms, pulling her arms to her sides and squinting. "I found these at Perlyn Hall yesterday." She lifted one paper and showed her sister. "Patience, you must know that it pains me to accept this as truth. However, you are in my care and I must warn you of what's to come if you continue down the path you have chosen." She tilted her palm upward and gestured over the papers from left to right. "These are each different headlines from major achievements in Mr. Williams' career, from his leaving England to crossing the Atlantic Ocean to returning from Africa. Every event is well documented for the public eye to behold."

Autumn swallowed, focusing on her sister, who didn't return her gaze.

"Don't you see? Each article highlights whatever is most important to him at the time, each set to be replaced by something of greater urgency upon his next appearance in print." She lifted the one announcing the engagement.

"Patience," Autumn's eyes welled with tears as her throat quivered, "As much as it pains me to admit it, you are just another one of the many, many achievements in this man's world." She handed her the headline, the paper shaking in her nervous fingers.

"So, this is why you were in his study yesterday? You weren't bringing him a pumpkin loaf but rather seeking to derail my heart from its fated course?"

"Patience, I swear I didn't mean to discover them. I stumbled upon all of this by accident."

"You really don't think he loves me, do you?"

"Oh, no, Patience, he loves you all right. He loves you as much as he loved his last success story. Look at his pride. You've always known him to be over joyous in celebrating his latest accomplishments. Right now, you are the centre of his world, his current headline. But like every other that came before, you will be inevitably replaced by some greater treasure.

"Just yesterday, you watched as he postponed showing you the observatory to discuss his world tour with the press. He will soon only speak of such forthcoming events and, once that is done, he will acquire the next headline, the next country, the next person..." Autumn squinted, sliding her hand into her ruffled sleeve and wiping at her dripping eyes. Her throat burned with the effort of speaking. "I am sure he will always love you with a decent sense of care, how could he not? You are a beautiful and charismatic young child with a precious soul that no man deserves. But I sincerely doubt someone of his character will suddenly change his ways. No, you are destined to become yesterday's headline to him and that I simply could not bear. Nor, I imagine, could you?"

"He would never put anything above myself..." Patience seemed to pose the response as more of a question.

"Do you think this is what I want? You must believe that I would give anything for Mr. Williams to be the perfect match for you. In fact, I would give up my own life this very instant if it meant your perfect happiness and safety with the suitor of your choice. You know I would. But Patience, do you really believe that you will be content to be a stepping stone in a never-ending line of accomplishments in this man's life?

"Wouldn't you rather be loved and cherished as the special creature you are? A wonderful, kind, caring human being deserving of so much more than he can offer. You are one of the rare few who are blessed with exceedingly great value. You cannot marry someone so unworthy of you."

Patience wetted the newspaper with her falling tears, sniffling and pursing her lips together. "There is still a possibility that you have mis-judged him."

"I am not attempting to deceive you but rather highlight the truth."

"I have to believe in him." Patience turned, still holding the paper as she fled up the stairs, her loud sobs starting once she reached the bedroom.

Autumn's heart hurt at her sister's pain. If only they didn't have to go on like this. Neither deserved such torment.

Autumn swallowed the lump in her throat and overturned her bag, sending the rest of the items inside sprawling across the newspapers on the low tabletop.

She moved her stiff fingers in and out to regain flexibility and picked up the envelope with the wax seal. If only Patience would come to her senses. Then she wouldn't have to post the letters. But, alas, her sister seemed determined not to change her mind. The letter was her only guarantee of saving her sister from her fate.

A small paper bag on the table came to Autumn's attention. She sighed, picking up the mystery parcel and unrolling the top section.

Autumn gasped, staring at the peanut brittle in her hand. That Mr. Foster! She ran her fingers along the bumpy patches on the treat as her face burned with the embarrassment of him having slipped something into her bag. And this of all things!

She shook her head, then marched outside, face fuming. She opened the front door and felt the cold air flooding in as she tossed out the brittle. There! She didn't have any extra time to wallow in her own tears anyhow! She must get the wax to Mr. Foster to assure her peace of mind.

And off she went, braving the misty morning with full force, crunching through the decaying leaves of the copse.

Little shrieks and giggles of children enjoying themselves pierced the air, lifting Autumn's soul despite herself.

She arrived in the luscious garden of the Raven's Nest, the spacious grass enclosed by a barrier of trees and stray bushes on all sides.

"Goodness!" Autumn pressed her palms against her chest, flinching at the sight of the three children whirling on teetering bicycles like lunatics under the blue sky. Mary-Elizabeth was riding with a strange man on a penny-farthing as Mr. Foster stood off to the side, near the home, listening to their play.

Autumn picked up her pace, careful not to be run over by the children as she sprinted through the grass. "Good morning, Mr. Foster." She approached him, her features hardening.

"Greetings, Miss Everleigh!"

She knitted her eyebrows together, bringing a troubled smile up one side of her mouth and curtsying, the shadow from the rooftops of the home causing her to shiver.

Mary-Elizabeth and the other man glided over on the four-foot-high wheel of the penny-farthing, slowing to a halt when they arrived.

"Good morning, madam," said the stranger, who wore dark trousers, a white button-up shirt, and suspenders. His thick black hair curled around his ears in little flurries.

"Miss Everleigh, this is Mr. Lawrence," said Mr. Foster.

"Pleasure to meet you. I cannot recall being in your presence before now...?"

"He is from Brampton. I have worked in his manor as a servant for... three years now, isn't that right, sir?" Mr. Foster faced his companion.

"Yes. Of course," Mr. Lawrence said, speaking slowly as he wiped the sweat from his dark brow.

Autumn gave a tight smile, darting her eyes between the two men. "Then, was it your idea, Mr. Lawrence, to bring these bicycles down here to secure ultimate disaster for these children?"

"It was mine, thank you," said Mr. Foster with a firm nod.

"I see." Autumn kept her tone stern. "Children—perhaps we should play something else now?" She glanced between each one and raised her eyebrows to signal their obedience.

"Must we?"

"I have already spoken with their parents," Mr. Foster piped up. "Mr. Glendale gave me permission to give them pleasure, and I'm afraid you cannot override his authority."

"They might fall!"

"They might. And if they do, we will tend to their needs."

Autumn scrunched up her face, fire pulsing through her veins.

"Let us head to the clearing near the brook, then," suggested Mr. Lawrence, peddling away. The children followed.

"You know," Mr. Foster stroked his chin, "You can't always live life in fear of losing what you possess. It would make gaining anything quite impossible."

"Thank you for sharing your thoughts with me. I am enriched by such wisdom."

"Come on," he said, face softening, "how will you know how to have fun if you never allow yourself to enjoy things?"

"I know perfectly well how to have fun, thank you very much!" Autumn tapped her foot and folded and unfolded her arms.

Mr. Foster bent his head, not able to conceal his smile.

"You don't believe me, do you?" Her voice betrayed her agitation despite her effort to keep her voice light.

"Perhaps you haven't experienced what true fun is."

"Clearly our ideas of fun are quite different."

Mr. Foster gripped the empty bicycle beside him. Much lower than the penny-farthing, both wheels were small and congruent.

"What exactly are you doing?"

"Riding!" And with that, he threw his leg over the seat and peddled on.

"Mr. Foster! You cannot see where you're going!" Horrified, Autumn put her hands over her face, parting some of her fingers to watch as he joined the group leaving the garden by way of the stone path.

"The wind is wonderful!" he called over his shoulder.

"You could kill yourself! Watch out for the bumps! Goodness what will you do when you fall?"

"Stand up and start again!"

"And if you are injured?"

He didn't answer as everyone went on laughing and smiling to themselves, oblivious to Autumn's distress.

"Be careful, Francis! Oh, do look out!" Her shouts were of no use. No one could hear above the fun.

"Not that I care!" She kicked at the grass. "I don't want anything to do with their dangerous cycling nonsense anyhow."

She hurried after everyone despite her annoyance, collecting her skirts and running to keep up. After all, someone had to watch and make sure the children were safe.

"What fun!" said Hazel as she peddled down the dirt road between the trees on either side.

"I am winning!" Mary-Elizabeth hollered from up high, stretching her little hands forward as far as they would go to touch the tips of the handlebars Mr. Lawrence held.

Mr. Foster, who travelled at the back of the group slowed to stop and hopped off his bicycle.

"All funned out, are we?" Autumn asked, the bottom of her dress caught up in her arms.

"Would you like to try? I'll show you how."

She swallowed, almost saying yes. But no, it was far too dangerous! She would be glad later when she returned home with all ten fingers and toes.

"With all due respect, I must refuse." She kicked at a pebble, sending the gravel against Mr. Foster's leg with a whack. If he noticed, he didn't mention it.

They all went down the path that led to an open plane of dirt surrounded by thick trees and a tiny stream.

"Miss Everleigh, would you hold this a moment?" Mr. Foster gave the bicycle a little shake.

She nodded, taking the handles as he raised a fist in the air and cheered, "Go, Hazel, go! Go, Francis, go! Go, Mary-Elizabeth, go!"

Autumn fixed her gaze on the empty bicycle. Maybe there was no real harm in trying once. She didn't have to like it. She could go slowly. Very, very slowly...

Autumn scanned the area to make sure no one was watching her. The children and Mr. Lawrence were all busy pedaling in circles. Mr. Foster, who stood off to the side, couldn't have seen her even if he wanted to. Good.

She set down her handbag and squeezed the handlebars, puffed air into her cheeks, and threw a leg over the seat.

I believe in you, she encouraged herself; whether the words were, in fact, true she refused to consider too carefully. She examined her situation with skepticism, sitting down and adjusting her skirts. Her heart catapulted vibrations through her insides, tempting her to retreat. No! All she had to do was lift one foot off the ground and go; simple! Ah, but that was the trickiest part. At least, so she assumed.

Autumn inhaled through her nostrils, kicked off the turf and tapped her boots around to find the pedals. She tipped to the wayside. *Oh!*

Her foot connected with the pedals, and she pushed down, heart in her mouth. The wheels moved a few inches. Her arms shook as she wobbled back and forth, keeping her eyes on the handlebars.

Not so bad. She placed a boot back in the dirt, her chest lifting and falling in swift movements. She hadn't moved very far, but that didn't matter, for if she could move three feet, then she could move a hundred.

Mr. Lawrence rode to Mr. Foster on wheels like butter and whispered something in his ear.

Autumn ignored them and attempted the contraption again, despite her blushes. She travelled a few feet, and the bike lurched to one side once more.

"Are you quite all right, Miss Everleigh?" asked Mr. Foster, coming over.

"Fine, fine..." she plowed her foot to the ground, preventing herself from toppling.

"Is anything the matter...?"

She swallowed, locking her eyes on a small yellow flower. She couldn't get off now, not when she was this far into riding it.

"I've, I've... never ridden before," she admitted, biting her lip, unable to face the man.

"Don't worry, I'll help you."

"I can do it myself."

"I know you can. I will just get you started."

Autumn agreed to this, so long as she decided how fast they went and when to slow down. After all, if she had control of when she started and stopped, then she couldn't fall, now could she?

"You see," he explained, "the trick is keeping your head in line with the wheels. Oh, and look up at where you're going, not down at the peddles. The faster you go, the easier it will be to keep your balance!"

He placed his fingers against her shoulders and ran his hand down her back until he found the seat. "I'll hold on while you get your speed up!"

Autumn's hand raised to grasp at her necklace but she soon thought better of it and gripped the handlebars.

"Go," he said.

She tightened her hold on the handles and pushed one foot down on the pedal, closing her eyes for a split-second before shooting them open.

The wind flew at her face as she picked up speed, rustling her hair and cooling her skin. She was in perfect control!

Autumn's insides did a summersault. "I love it!" she squealed, dragging her boots into the dirt once more.

"Well done!" Mr. Foster called from way back. "You were doing so well! You didn't even need me!"

A low laugh of utter delight soon became a light giggle. Well then, this wasn't as bad as she had thought! Still risky, of course. Something she only needed to do once or twice, but exhilarating nonetheless! Besides, she could keep herself balanced on her own. She was in control.

Autumn turned her bicycle around and joined the children, smiling.

"Autumn!" Francis' jaw dropped. "You're riding a bicycle!"

"Don't shout so!" She led the group in a circle, smiling and inhaling the fresh fall breeze. What bliss! What fun! The beautiful brightness combined with the wind from riding made quite the experience indeed. She imagined the sun was her sister and the wind herself; together they brightened the day.

"Francis, watch out!" Hazel panicked, swerving toward her brother.

"You're in my way!" The two children collided head on with one another, their vehicles tipping, and both siblings crashed to the ground.

"Oh!" Autumn released the pedals, coasting to a slow stop. She threw one leg over the seat and hopped on the other.

"Do either of you feel any pain?" she called urgently, running to their sides. Mr. Foster followed her.

"Hazel..." Francis groaned, standing to his feet and brushing off his dirty shins. "What happened?"

"It's all your fault!" She stood, sticking out her tongue. "You were in my way."

"Let me see," Autumn bent down and took Hazel's arm, running her fingers over her skin and searching for any blood.

"I am fine," the girl pulled away. "Only a few scratches."

"Same," added Francis, standing up his bicycle and dusting off the seat.

"Thank goodness." Autumn sniffed, wiping at her wet eyes. "This is exactly the kind of accident I was worried about!"

Mr. Lawrence rode over with Mary-Elizabeth. "We should probably be heading back about now anyway. Are you coming, Kendrick?"

"Of course," answered Mr. Foster.

"At last." Autumn nodded and beckoned for the children to follow. They climbed back on their bicycles and pedalled away after Mr. Lawrence.

"I shall await your apology for nearly killing Francis and Hazel," Autumn said to Mr. Foster as she collected her bag and took the vehicle by the handlebars, giving the entire thing a good shake.

"That's a bit extreme."

Autumn had to agree to some extent. "If they had died, it would have been all your fault."

"They didn't die."

"They could have, and therefore I'm still very displeased with you. Well. A little displeased..." She waited for him to argue with her, but his manner remained mild and pleasant.

"On the bright side, you loved riding."

"Hah!" She kicked at a stick lying on the road. "I did not *love* riding. I... enjoyed it. A little. There's a difference, isn't there?"

Mr. Foster couldn't hide his smile now, and he made Autumn's pride burn.

"Okay, fine!" She tossed one of her hands up in the air and let it fall against her skirts. "I will admit that I enjoyed it quite a bit. I would do it again, given decent circumstances. Maybe. And I mean maybe. Are you happy now?"

"Indubitably."

"It's still improper. And it's very, very dangerous, of course."

"Of course." He nodded, still smiling.

She decided to abandon this subject, lest she come across as too thrilled on the matter, and opened her handbag. "I brought you the wax for the stamp. I meant to give it to you last night but I forgot." She held the envelope out with the precious wax so that the corner pressed against his gloved wrist.

"Wonderful! I'll be sure to work on it when I return to Brampton tomorrow." He took the paper from her hands and stuffed it into his pocket as they walked, the children and Mr. Lawrence now out of view.

"How many days will it take for you to finish?"

"A few."

"Then you will expect to see more of me in the coming week to be sure you haven't forgotten. And do be extra careful with the wax. I only have the one."

"Of course."

Autumn's heart raced as she ran forward to kick at a stray pile of coloured leaves. The bits of foliage fluttered into the air, sprinkling across her body as she kept walking. "I am going to miss this weather." She squeezed her eyelids shut and breathed in through her nose. What bliss!

"You know," said Mr. Foster, "there is a fragrance in autumn that you simply don't find in any other season."

"Yes, and one has the opportunity to make leaf angels!" She leaned the bicycle against a nearby tree, sank into a nice big collection of fallen leaves, and moved her arms up and down while squinting from the sunlight. My, she would miss fall with its pretty orange and red clusters. But of course, there were always snow angels come winter, and those could be even better, so long as you were careful not to catch a chill.

"So?" she asked when she stood to her feet and brushed at the dirt on her skirts. "Kendrick, huh?"

"Ah, a name few have called me, I'm afraid. But that will soon change, for the world may one day know me as Kendrick A. Foster. My publishing name."

"And may I ask what you are working on now, Kendrick A. Foster?" She bent down and scooped an armful of leaves and let them sift over his unsuspecting head.

"Hey!" He spat the leaves from his mouth and brushed his face.

"Just a little *fun*," she teased. She turned away and touched her teeth together, taking the bicycle in her hands. "And you deserved it, anyway."

"How so?" He scowled, pulling a twig from his hair.

"For making me ride a bicycle against my will, putting Hazel's and Francis' lives in terrible jeopardy and for... whatever horrors you have in store for me next."

"I shall try and improve my behaviour. To answer your question, I am currently working on improving my descriptions of being underwater, a night under a full moon, and... well, dancing."

"Yes," Autumn said, growing quiet. She had done her best to describe dancing, whether he liked her verbal picture of the matter or not.

"Underwater is a land full of cloud and mist," she said. "The waters are a wonder of sensation and mystery, like seeing the enemy seconds before he strikes. Beneath the water, the world is like a dreamscape, real life shimmering somewhere above the surface."

"Quite atmospheric, though would you say it's more like a controlled dream? You are still aware of the outside world, yet it seems so distant in comparison?"

"Yes, that's it. How funny. Controlled dreaming is a description I used once in a story I made up for my sister. Many years ago."

"She must mean a lot to you."

Autumn wheeled the bicycle along, lowering her tone. "Oh, the world. It's why I am so upset that she—" Autumn pushed a stray piece of hair behind her ear and kicked at the ground, "that she's intent on marrying Mr. Williams."

"What did he do?"

"Nothing. Well, not really. It's just…" she swallowed, suddenly tearful. "I spent my entire life protecting and nourishing her, and yet she pledges to simply throw my love away." Mr. Foster would never understand. No one would.

"She doesn't realise all you have sacrificed for her. You must have taken truly excellent care of her."

Autumn cocked her head, looked into his big brown eyes, and sniffed. "Yes… that's, that's exactly it, which is why I need to make the stamp. If I can just show her what's important, she will change."

"Miss Patience is lucky to have a sister like you in her life."

Autumn put two fingers under her eye and cleaned up the tears forming in the crevices. "You… you really think so?"

"Sure. Love is rare and doesn't come to the undeserving. I speak from experience. No one respects, let alone dares to love, me."

"They don't?"

"No."

"How can you be certain?"

"When I went blind, I was in my early twenties. I was of low class, and the relationships I cherished vanished like the black of night come dawn as they deemed me useless, unable to secure a stable source of wealth that would meet their expectations.

"I later inherited my great uncle's riches, and my social status quickly changed. While men and companies still scoffed at my shortcomings, they withdrew their comments when informed of my assets and proceeded to treat me as a king."

"How awful of these people to act in such a cruel fashion. If I may inquire, however did you respond to their harsh judgment?"

"By giving them all I possessed and becoming poor again."

"How could you do such a thing?"

"Money only changes how others see you. Why should I be praised for my wealth when I could, instead, risk being loved for who I am on the inside? Admiration for one's fortune cannot compare to the treasured praise of the heart. And once I show them my published article in the paper, they will see a different side of me. They will no longer scoff."

"And who are 'they'?"

Mr. Foster scratched his chin as if he had he never thought about the question before. "Everyone," he said after a pause. "Everyone."

"And is Mr. Glendale publishing you in his paper? That would be rather convenient for you."

"Of a sort. I have previously been all over the country trying to get printing houses to pick up my work. Everyone thus far has turned me down. They don't want a blind man associated with their establishment, I suppose, which I can understand. This led me to Mr. Glendale, who reached out to me not for my writing but for my accounting career. Of course, I saw this as an opportunity and offered my services in return for a single page in his paper to display one of my works and full name. He has given me until Christmas to compose the article. If I don't finish in time, I doubt I will ever have a chance like this again."

Autumn smiled, taking pity on the poor man. She had never seen this side of him before. "I shall very much like to have a copy of the paper when it is finished."

"Would you?"

"Most definitely."

They soon arrived back at the Raven's Nest to find the children's bicycles lying haphazardly in the backyard and no one in sight. *Gone off to play inside, no doubt,* Autumn thought.

"I suppose this is where we part," said Mr. Foster.

"Indeed. I shall expect you to take good care of the seal in my absence."

"Of course. You have my permission to check in as often as you wish." And he turned, heading toward the house.

Autumn pulled at the tips of her sleeve, swallowing. Before he was out of earshot, she spoke "Mr. Foster," she said softly. "I think—I mean, I *know* you are deserving of love."

Mr. Foster stopped and turned, half-smiling. "If only you could get the rest of the world to think so, too."

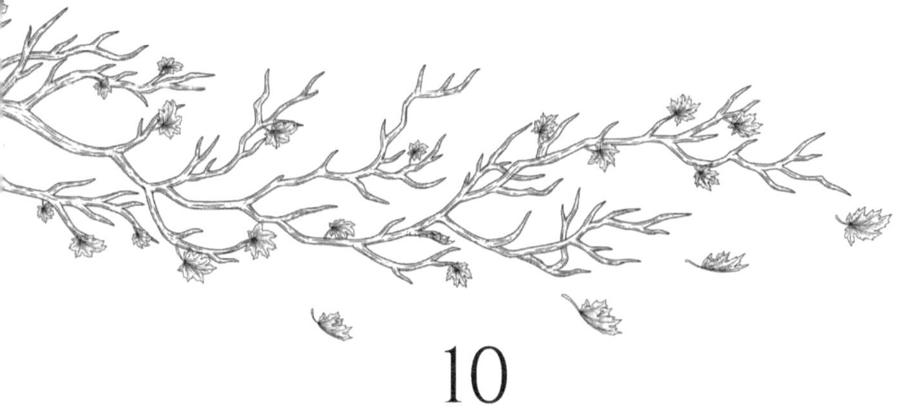

10

Autumn went down to the cellar to gather the rest of the apples, hoping they hadn't gone rotten by now. The days were already getting colder and extra layers and thicker gloves were needed, so it only made sense to make some fresh apple cider before winter arrived.

It was a tradition that the sisters make the drink together every year, something they had done as children with their mother. Though Autumn and her sister weren't speaking now, she could at least bring Patience some of the beverage.

She truly loved making apple cider. It was heartwarming to sit in one's kitchen, stirring the pot and breathing in the rich fragrance. The tasting was by far the best part. After all, how would she to know how much sugar was the right amount if she didn't first sample the drink a dozen or so times? It had to be extra sweet, for that was how Patience liked it best. Double the sugar! This year would be no different from previous years, except she wouldn't have her sister by her side helping her.

Autumn carried the last crate of apples up the steps and into the kitchen. After washing her hands, she began chopping the fruit. These were the best kind of apples, straight from the Pickerly farm. That was one perk of occasionally helping there; they were kept well stocked in fresh produce.

After she had cleaned her knife with a cloth, Autumn set to work. The entire time, she thought only of her pretty sister.

Autty, this is delicious! Patience's words echoed in her mind as she remembered snuggling close together this time last year.

Autumn shook the memory out of her thoughts, pulled out a large pot, stoked the fire, and set the pot to boil. She slid her knife against the cutting board to guide the fruit into the simmering water below, covered the pot, and waited.

While she waited, she wiped the countertops and attempted to scrub the smudgy oven. The wonderful scents of apple wafted through the kitchen, caressing her senses. Autumn smiled at the smell as she lifted her cleaning rag to the oven. Without warning, tears came to her eyes. She curled up on the cold floor, her head in her hands, her back against a cabinet, her lungs throbbing. She wept for the hundredth time in days.

How could she ever have made this cider without her sister? She was no longer angry with Patience. Perhaps she had been at first, but now, she just wanted her back. This confrontation wasn't worth the pain; nothing was. The last few times they had spoken were brief but not angry. Why, she had seen emotion in Patience's big eyes when they had spoken in the hall just the other day; she too must want an end to this.

In her heart, Autumn knew that she had forgiven her sister, even if she couldn't accept her behaviour. If only they could address their feelings frankly. If only Patience would accept Mr. Williams as a scandal and move on.

After the cider had boiled a while, Autumn took a giant spoon and mashed the fruit. The smells filled her nostrils, filled the entire house now. Her eyes stung.

Once she found a mesh to drain out the chunks, she was ready for the best part; adding as much sugar as possible and serving the cider with cinnamon sticks.

"Patience!" Autumn called with a soft tone once she was satisfied with her brew.

Nothing.

"Patience!" she called again.

There was a dull thud from upstairs and, after a moment, Patience entered the kitchen. She looked miserable.

"I made hot apple cider." Autumn gave a faint smile and raised the tray with two steaming mugs.

Their eyes locked as they stood in silence. In pain. In heartbreak, their gazes parallel and in correspondence with the other. Sharing the same burden.

Autumn had to close her eyes lest she cry, and she extended the tray in hopes of encouraging her sister to take the drink.

"Oh. No, thank you." Patience burst into tears and tore back up the stairs, crying all the way.

Autumn's face crumpled as she jostled the tray, sending a trickle of cider running down her arms.

"What did I do wrong?" She wept, arms shaking but still grasping the tray as a few drops of liquid spilled onto her dress. The tears felt like tiny flames on her face as she swallowed at the fiery lump lurking in the back of her throat. How could she enjoy the apple cider now?

More of the liquid washed over her.

Autumn didn't care. She set down the tray, then gripped the walls as she hobbled to the front door, still crying.

Hunched over, she stumbled outside. The cold air scalded her puffy eyes and pushed her away from the house and down the front path.

The temperature had already started to drop in the evenings, and the cold lasted long into the morning, with ice particles frosted on the ground and the birds nestling into the bare, hollow trees. Soon, it may even snow.

Autumn rubbed at her arms as her teeth chattered.

Life will be normal again soon, she told herself. She would have her sister and could once again start saving for that dream house of hers. The home... what a blessing it would be. For some reason, the thought of that house didn't please her as much now as it did before.

The wind roared in Autumn's ears, sending stray leaves fluttering.

"Oh!" She clasped her face with her hands and shut her eyes as something slapped against her face.

"Oh!" She stepped back and swatted at her cheeks. With courage, she opened her eyes. A small envelope fluttered at her nose, flapping and crinkling in the breeze.

"Oh!" She laughed, reaching up to grab the item. As she clasped the paper in her fingers, a gust of wind tore the envelope from her hold.

She ran after it, jumping and stretching out her arms in attempts to capture the prize.

So close! Her fingers made contact with the tip of the paper.

She lunged at it again, missing. The paper swooped upward, waving one corner as if saying goodbye before sweeping into the depths of the copse.

Autumn paced in and out of the trees, confident the envelope would be caught on something or amongst the trees.

Then she spotted it; the envelope had flown high and caught in some branches.

"Got you!"

Autumn jumped and snatched the paper. "You are a naughty little thing, aren't you?" she whispered playfully as she turned it over in her hands.

Her eyebrows knitted together. She squinted at the red wax on the envelope. Mr. Williams' seal. How on earth had this gotten out here? She examined the front and back side. This was hers... the very same one she had given to Mr. Foster. He had lost it! Oh, she knew she couldn't trust that forgetful, careless man. She had been such a fool!

Autumn drew in a long breath and headed for the Raven's Nest. Arriving, she stormed into the home with frozen fingers, a pounding heart, and a desire to catch her breath, but that could come later—after she gave Mr. Foster a piece of her mind!

To her surprise, the door gaped open on the vacant office, allowing cold wind to gush across the threshold and into the hall.

She stepped in to find papers fluttering all around in the room, slapping against the desk and walls like a hundred butterflies set free.

"Goodness!" She clasped one of the pieces and glanced at the numbers written on it. These must be important!

She collected another and another, wrinkling most by mistake as she gathered as many as she could carry.

"Oh, no, you don't!" Several escaped from her arms, including the one with the seal, and re-entered the air with glee.

The window!

She clutched the papers against her chest, bending over to keep them from falling, and reached the open window. She shut the blasted thing before it could do any more damage.

"Goodness." Her chest heaved as she closed her eyes. That Mr. Foster. He almost ruined everything!

She relocated her special envelope resting on the floor and lifted it to her mouth to kiss the seal.

Autumn went to find the children and asked them if they knew where Mr. Foster was.

They all shook their heads no.

Autumn soon found Mrs. Glendale and asked her.

"Why, he went back to his estate in Brampton, dear." And the lady gave her directions.

Autumn thanked her and headed home to collect some winter garments for the walk to Brampton. She would make Mr. Foster finish her stamp today and she would give him a piece of her mind, too. That way she could post the letters in the morning. She'd have her relationship with Patience restored before long and soon they'd drink cider together and be at peace once again.

She collected her things and went on her way.

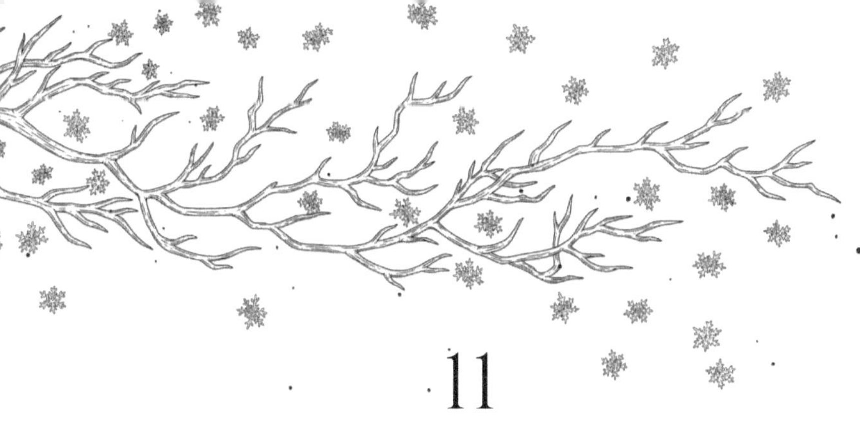

11

Autumn neared Brampton and tugged at her cloak with gloved hands. There were two thoughts in her mind. First was the Winter Ball, which she dreaded, since she knew that Patience would beg her to go, despite Autumn refusing to dance and associate with men for simple pleasure, regardless of what society thought of her. The second thought was of *A Christmas Carol*, the play.

For the past five or so years, Autumn had taken her sister to see a live performance of *A Christmas Carol* at the end of November. They had to travel to the outskirts of Carlisle by way of carriage. It was the only time of year that Autumn agreed to ride, since they couldn't walk so far in the weather. The train was, of course, unthinkable.

However, unlike the Winter Ball, the theatre was something Autumn loved ever so much. To sit in the red-velvet chair snuggled close to

Patience, eating popcorn and drinking cocoa, all while watching the performers below! If only she could be one of the ghosts of Christmas past, present, or future. Which would be best? Certainly not present. Past? Yes, for she could always go back to a time when she and her sister were happy.

What a shame, thought Autumn. They wouldn't see the show this year, despite the fact she had already purchased tickets. She couldn't possibly go now, not with her and her sister upset with each other. Missing the wonderful tradition would be heartbreaking.

Autumn shivered and squinted at the sky. Snow had to be around the corner. Just look at those clouds.

After nearly an entire afternoon of walking in the cold, Autumn arrived at the silver gates of Mr. Foster's residence.

An uneven brick path greeted her feet, guiding her to a tall marble fountain; its centrepiece was double her height and trickling gently. How beautiful! Autumn lifted her dress and seated herself on the smooth edge, gazing down. She took off her white gloves to dip her fingers in and tap her reflection, sending her face into ripples.

She drew her eyes away from the water and squeezed her arms against her chest, catching sight of the manor down the path. The building sat amongst various hills. Thick towers of many shapes and sizes decorated the structure of elegant brick. If Autumn hadn't known better, she might have guessed it to be a castle left over from medieval times. In fact, maybe it was a castle, one that had been added on to throughout the years, with the mix of slanted and cone roofs with tall spires.

She started the long, winding walk to the entrance, shivering as she glanced between the hills and the impressive home, wind tugging her hair loose.

"The Ivory," she whispered, reading the golden letters above the archway as she climbed the front steps. The name certainly couldn't be referring to the colour of the building, for it was grey rather than cream or white. Perhaps it referred to the interior or even the fountain in front. Mr. Foster couldn't possibly live here! It was too grand! She must have been directed to the wrong place.

Autumn lifted a hand to the knocker and gave a few thumps.

The door creaked open instantly.

"Hello," said a servant from within.

"Hello," she answered in awe, eyes shifting to the inside. "I'm here to see Mr. Foster."

The servant looked her over, as if trying to guess whether she spoke the truth or not. "Have you a calling card?"

"No, sir, I am here on business... with his express permission." She took a step in, the warmth of the inside exhilarating on her body.

"You may follow," said he, though he was frowning.

"Of course..." she said breathlessly as her gaze shifted to the inside of the home. The first room was an open cylindrical shape, decked in thick pillars running along the textured walls with golden trimmed edges and a domed ceiling. How wonderful it would be to sing in the middle and absorb the echoes from above!

The servant beckoned for her to follow him into a hall larger than Autumn's entire house. It was three stories high and paved with reflective checkered tiles. Candlesticks and the fading light from the windows lit the framed paintings, each depicting a scene of gayety and leisure.

She proceeded up a carpeted flight of stairs displaying two separate balconies, each with its own archway decorated with statues in niches in the walls.

"In here," said the servant, directing her to another room.

She kept her gaze on the hall, not wanting to leave, but did as she was told.

"I will go and find Mr. Foster," he told her, and he left.

She stepped into the space she had been escorted to and her heart stopped. Floor-to-ceiling windows made up three of the four walls, each with curtains open to allow the sun to bathe the room in vibrant goodness. A thick, white rug dressed the clean wooden floor. Golden armchairs with teal cushions and stools gathered around two grand pianofortes. Sister pianofortes!

Autumn closed her eyes and inhaled. It was as if she were paying a visit to the sun itself.

"Hello, sun!" She kept her eyes shut and spread her arms wide, spinning in circles to soak in as much of the room as possible. She giggled in bliss, the hem of her modest dress swirling as she spun.

"I certainly didn't expect to hear your voice today."

Autumn stopped spinning and turned to face the door, her face lit with laugher as she shook her dizzy head, dress catching up a moment too late and twisting around her body.

"Are you displeased by my presence?" she asked, furrowing her brows while turning her mouth down and cocking her head, waiting for something encouraging to come from his lips.

"No, not at all," he replied in haste. "I am merely surprised. But it's a good kind of surprise. The kind where your afternoon was dull and you weren't anticipating anything out of the ordinary to happen, but then something comes along the moment you least expect it to and changes the route of your day."

"A fork in the road." Autumn smiled.

"Exactly."

"Ah, but which path shall you take, Mr. Foster?" she laughed. It felt good to laugh. Laughing was something she seldom did, even when she and Patience were getting along smoothly. That said, it was usually Patience who provided her with an excuse for laughter. Last month, for example, when the sisters were painting pictures of pumpkins and Patience spilled most of the paint all over herself and Autumn. They had both chuckled and finished their paintings with much more energy so that each ended up having an extra splash of colour where the paint had splattered.

"It's a sort of modern art, maybe," Patience had said with a blush.

"If modern art is a rainbow, then I suppose," Autumn had giggled.

"So," she said, bringing her thoughts back into the present as she tugged at the tips of her gloves. "You have a very lovely home."

Mr. Foster scratched his neck. "Mr. Lawrence does have a lovely home, yes."

"Is it his?"

"Yes. Yes, it is. Somewhat grand, I daresay. I am fortunate enough to be staying here on occasions such as today."

"Somewhat grand? No, far more than merely grand. It's a palace! I should think anyone lucky for living here."

Mr. Foster didn't speak right away. He tapped his leg a few times and turned his face toward the windows. Thinking of his writing no doubt.

"I assume you're here for a reason?"

"Oh! Oh, yes!" She reached for her bag. She had forgotten why she had come in the midst of her pleasure. "You left your office window open, and my precious seal flew out into the breeze. You are ever so lucky I found it, or it would have been lost forever."

His mouth fell open, and he slapped his forehead, mumbling something under his breath she couldn't quite make out.

"My goodness! Miss Everleigh, I am a fool. Forgive me, if I could ever earn such an honour."

Autumn couldn't bring herself to scold him as she had planned. After all, there was no real harm done. She was sure he wouldn't make the same mistake again.

"No, no, it's quite all right. At least you have it now."

"I will finish as soon as I possibly can. I shall start tonight."

Autumn nodded. "In that case, I suppose I should..."

"If you wish to remain a while, I would be more than delighted to show you the sights of the mansion. I am sure Mr. Lawrence wouldn't mind."

Autumn swallowed and glanced around the room. "Thank you for the offer, but I should let you get on with your work. Is the man at home today? I should like to bid him farewell upon my departure."

"No, he is out."

"A pity. Please do wish him my best regards on his return."

"Of course."

She brushed her dress.

"You may escort me to the door, if you wish." Secretly, she desired to stay longer and spin in that beautiful room. Maybe she should have said yes to a tour.

Mr. Foster turned and started toward the exit. Autumn frowned. "Arm?"

"I beg your forgiveness, yet again." He extended his elbow, and she placed her hand on his arm as they left. She couldn't help glancing from left to right as they went, hoping to catch a glimpse into some of the other gorgeous rooms. She did succeed in seeing a large painting of dancers and singers, with a frame from floor to ceiling, taking up an entire wall.

"My coat and scarf," said Mr. Foster when they reached the entry. Two servants appeared almost instantly to present him with a top hat, scarf, and coat. "Let us be on our way," he said, pulling the scarf around his neck.

"Where to?" Autumn asked.

"To the Raven's Nest, of course. I have errands to run anyway."

Autumn didn't object to this and took his arm once more.

They left the estate and arrived in the town of Brampton to find a bustle of energy. Carriages whirled about, while dozens of citizens carried packages of fresh goods. Some folk stood way up on tall ladders or in store windows, setting up the holiday displays. Christmas was only a month away, and no one hesitated to keep the marketplace booming. Pine-branch garlands already lined the lampposts, topped off with glimmering red bows. The crisp scent of peppermint flooded the streets as the aromas of fresh treats whirled out the door of a nearby bakery.

Autumn drew in her breath, her cheeks rosy. So much to see and hear! Decorations, smells, even music from the small band of carolers on the street corner dressed in warm attire. They smiled when Autumn and Mr. Foster walked by, and she nodded in return. The entire scene before her made her recall one of her favourite poems. From what she remembered, it went something a little like,

"Pine needle branches, cold and lush, breathed scents of crimson into a blush.

Snug in a corner, oh ever so near, a pale old man shed a lonely tear.

He had no comfort on this cold night but a couple of mice, and a store window's light.

I extended a hand and said with a quiver, "Merry Christmas to you. May I help with your shiver?"

From my small pocket, I produced a treat. A mere morsel, but it smoked with heat.

The man gave a nod and whispered with joy, "You are a wonder. God bless you, my boy."

Autumn liked that poem. The only thing missing now was the snow. Perhaps it would snow soon. Today must be the coldest day of the year. She had overheard Mr. Pundson talking at the market yesterday, saying to a customer,

"Yes sir, George, snow isn't far off. I can feel it in my bones. And they are never wrong."

Autumn wholeheartedly believed him. Who was she to disagree? She had purchased eggs from the man every week for as long as she could remember, and she for one was as confident in his weather-predicting abilities as he was himself. His only real flaw was rubbing it in the faces of the doubters when his predictions came true.

Autumn stared now as they walked past a toy shop. Children rushed in and pulled their frayed parents by the hands with smiles spread across their faces.

"I hope Father Christmas brings me the doll I want!" A little girl pointed to the window display housing various toys and trinkets cluttered around a book with a red cover. *A Christmas Carol.*

Autumn gave a faint smile, wishing she was still going to the play with her sister that year.

"Do you have any plans for the holidays?" Mr. Foster spoke, breaking into Autumn's thoughts. He had been rather quiet since they'd left the Ivory.

"Been stuck in your head once again?" she inquired, turning her attention away from the display as they walked.

"Yes, my mind got away with me," said he. "Let us go right. A shortcut." And they did.

Autumn went back to the question. "I would certainly enjoy a quaint little Christmas with my sister, if the Lord allows."

"And why wouldn't He?"

"Well. Patience and I are upset with one another, remember? And we usually go to see a performance of *A Christmas Carol* every year. Have you been?"

"I can't say that I have. Is it grand?"

"Is it grand?" She said with such a gasp that she stumbled forward, losing her balance and hopping on one foot.

"Grand," she exhaled, clutching his arm and locking her eyes on his, "does not even begin to describe it! We always go to the Bronzewood theatre. It's massive! You first go inside and purchase refreshments. Hot chocolate, the real kind made from melted chocolate, not the bland powdery stuff from the general stores. Next, candied popcorn. Five different flavours to choose from! I always get buttered, and Patience chooses caramel. After that, we are escorted to the theatre. They have so many rows, that fit hundreds of guests. And there are these beautiful little boxes, high, high up, where you can sit by yourselves and use the opera glasses to see the stage! Oh, I've always wanted to sit in one of those. But I've never had the money."

Mr. Foster kept smiling and nodded.

"Then there's the show itself!" She gave his arm a good hard squeeze. "There are so many actors! Of course, there is Scrooge... You are familiar with the story, aren't you?" She looked at Mr. Foster keenly.

"I know a little, although my knowledge perhaps is a bit rusty."

"I will fill in the gaps, then! Ebenezer Scrooge is this wicked old man who cares about nothing more than his own filthy fortune, and you see, on Christmas Eve, he is visited by three spirits!" Autumn went on, not even paying attention to where they were going.

"Two, please," Mr. Foster said as they came to a stop at a window. Autumn continued with vigour.

"And my favourite part is how Patience snuggles up close to me while we watch together and it feels like paradise—are you listening?"

"Have a good day, sir," he said and turned to Autumn. "Yes, I am listening."

"Where are we?" She bit her lip and examined the unfamiliar location, hollow and full of noise with people scurrying about carrying bits and pieces of luggage.

"A shortcut, as I told you earlier. Remember?"

Autumn raised her brows and nodded slowly before continuing, "And then, after the show, we always get some popcorn to take home."

"It sounds wonderful," he chuckled.

"Oh, it is!" She smiled. However, her bright expression faded as she looked at the ground. "Except... we're not going this year."

"May I ask why not?"

She sighed. Perhaps talking about Patience would help her feel less disappointed. Besides, Mr. Foster had proven to be a better listener than she'd anticipated.

"I purchased tickets to the show. But, as I have already told you, Patience and I are not speaking with one another. Oh, how I wish we were! I do believe neither of us is truly upset anymore, but I don't know what to do." She waited for him to say something like "That's too bad," or "Maybe next year." Instead, he said nothing. "The worst part is that this is our family tradition. We've gone for several years, now."

He still said nothing.

Autumn cocked her head and bit her lip. "Goodness me, are you well, Mr. Foster?"

"Go," he said with a firm tone.

"What?"

"Go with your sister to the theatre." He spoke as if what he said were obvious.

"Oh, but I simply can't. It's so complicated. Besides, she would never want to come with me!"

"When you look back one year on from now, are you going to be sad you missed it or glad it happened? One situation can change a lot about a person."

"Yes, well, you see—"

"Don't let anything override the love you have for her. Anything."

Autumn ran her fingers through her hair.

"I- I- I can't," she said, lips trembling. A tear escaped as she shuddered. Of course, she wanted to go! More than anything. Not because of the popcorn or fancy dancers or the beautiful building and Christmas decorations but because of the memories she made with her sister.

"What's the worst thing that could happen?" he asked.

"I ask her to come, and she says no."

"And what if she says yes?"

"We might not have a good time!"

"And what's the best that could happen?"

"She says, 'yes, of course we're going,' and we have a wonderful time…"

He pulled his arm away from hers. "Sometimes we can be so focused on the wrongdoings of the other person that we forget our own part of the equation."

Autumn had never thought of it that way before. "I'll do it," she mumbled.

"Well, at least sound happy about it."

"I'll do it!" She laughed. "Thank you." She lifted her head high and followed Mr. Foster deeper into the building with high arched ceilings and a big clock suspended from above, wondering where this shortcut was taking them.

"What about you?" she said, taking his arm again, although her mind was somewhat distant. Either the air was growing foggier or she was become lightheaded with excitement. Perhaps it was a mixture of both. "Do you have any plans?"

"Not particularly. We plan to decorate a little. I always love putting up the tree. It smells so wonderful! Pine, roasted chestnuts, cinnamon."

How awful it must be, thought Autumn, *to not see Christmas! No snow, no gifts. Only feeling and smelling. And tasting.* This caused her mind to drift to her favourite winter treats; hot cocoa, peppermint sticks, ginger biscuits. She recalled one year in particular when she and Patience had accidentally made triple the gingerbread batter and almost destroyed the oven! Afterward, the piece was so big, that it practically toppled over altogether.

"Miss Everleigh," said Mr. Foster quietly. "You aren't going to like this."

"Oh?" She knitted her brow as she studied Mr. Foster's face.

"All aboard!" a loud voice boomed, echoing across the long-arched tunnel.

Autumn only now grasped her surroundings. She was standing indoors on a large platform, crowded with a flurry of people piling into large red train cars with smoke rolling over her feet.

"Oh! Absolutely not!" She stepped back, bumping against a pillar and fingering her necklace.

"Miss Everleigh, hear me out," said Mr. Foster as he reached out a hand as if to secure her but quickly drew back.

"No, I won't go! You... you can't make me!"

"You're right." He nodded. "I cannot make you."

"Oh?"

"And even if you did ride, you would obviously be in complete control."

"Would I?" She shook her head and let out a huff. "How am I to be in control of a moving train exactly?"

"There's a lever. One in every cabin. If you don't like the ride, you pull it, and the train stops at your command."

Autumn frowned. She hadn't known of this lever before.

"Believe me," said he, "when I say that nothing of beauty has ever come from a place of complete comfort."

She squeezed her eyes shut and scrunched up her face.

"All aboard!" called the conductor as steam puffed from the exhaust of the shiny smokestack.

Autumn popped her eyes open and let her gaze settle on the cursive letters painted on the side of the engine: *The A. & P. Express.*

Her eyebrows furrowed. *Autumn and Patience...*

"Last call!" The conductor held up his chained watch and tapped his foot, mustache twitching.

Autumn took one last look at the platform and tightened her arm muscles. She had survived a ride on a bicycle. If she could do that, why not this? After all, she was in control.

"Well, you don't want to miss our ride, do you?" she clasped Mr. Foster's hand and bolted for the train.

Goodness! What was she doing? She could be injured, killed, or worse!

A smile swept over her face, despite these fears, and a sensation of energy ignited in her chest. She didn't recognise the person inside her who made the choice to board—for it certainly couldn't be Autumn Everleigh! Yet, the girl inside felt vaguely familiar, almost as if they had met before...

Poor Mr. Foster's eyes were bloodshot as if he, too, was surprised by her actions. But as she helped him to board, his face morphed into delight.

Autumn took in a huge breath and stepped into the first car.

"Mr. Foster!" boomed the friendly voice of an attendant inside.

"Mr. Hopkins!" Mr. Foster reached forward, fumbling around until he shook the fellow's hand.

"There are plenty of available seats," the man assured them. "Take any of your liking."

Autumn nodded, not giving him another glance as she walked down the aisle, eyes searching for this "lever" she had been promised. Ah, there! She nodded to it.

Several rows of soft seats with wooden armrests lined the car with luggage compartments, carpet, stained glass, and three large crystal chandeliers.

Every row displayed two seats and a window, the left side looking out on a brick wall and on the right, the station.

How luxurious!

Autumn faced Mr. Foster, who couldn't conceal his grin.

"Oh, honestly. Wipe that look off your face this instant!" she hissed with a hint of laughter. She was giddy with nerves.

He chuckled, shaking his head from side to side. "I am sorry, it's just that this isn't the Miss Everleigh I knew only this morning. That's all."

A piercing whistle thundered through her ears as the car chugged forward.

"Oh!" Autumn shrieked, slapping her hands against her armrests and causing everyone around her to give a rather curious glance in her direction.

The train slowly picked up speed and pulled out of the station, the brick wall transitioning into a grassy view.

Autumn brought her right hand to her neck, tapped her skin until she found the ring on the chain around her neck, and ran her fingers up and down the smooth surface. She shuddered as someone tapped her on the shoulder.

Mr. Foster's voice was gentle, "It's going to be all right."

"I should never have done this." Autumn's voice was small and quiet.

The doors at the far end of the cabin burst open and in paced several men pushing carts of refreshments.

"Anything to drink, miss?" an attendant asked Autumn. "Wine, tea?"

Autumn puffed up her cheeks, putting a hand across her mouth. "Not unless you would like me to regurgitate whatever I consume all over you and the rugs, thank you very much. If you do, then be my guest." And she sank her head in her hands and shut her eyes.

Mr. Foster leaned forward and whispered to the server,

"I'll take a whisky, if you don't mind."

Autumn groaned. She should never have settled for this. Why, this was awful! Terrible! She despised it! More than anything.

Mr. Foster must have sensed her anguish, for he said, "Look," and tapped his hand on her shoulder once more. "You are missing the view."

She frowned and gave a quick glance at the rocky peaks on the far side of the valley. How pretty!

"Wow," she said under her breath.

"What do you see? The mountains, or the town?"

"The mountains," she said with an exhale.

"I've been told they are beautiful. What do you think of them?"

Autumn laughed. "Beautiful can't even begin to describe them."

"And how should you begin to describe them?"

"As—"

"Ticket, ma'am?" interrupted a man with glasses and a notepad.

"Oh!" Autumn touched her dress and dug through her bag as if the ticket would be there.

"Here you are, sir." Mr. Foster held his drink in one hand and passed two papers over with the other.

The man took them, stamped each, and handed them back.

"When did you buy those?" Autumn demanded once he left.

"While you were telling me about *A Christmas Carol*," explained Mr. Foster.

"Oh," Autumn nodded, trying to remember when that would have been.

The train gave a small jerk as if hitting something small on the tracks and kept going.

"Ah!" she shrieked, drawing the attention of everyone around her once again. She didn't care if they thought her crazy! Let them stare. She held the ring on her necklace in her fist and let out little moans and groans. In the back of her mind, she recalled a newspaper article about a train crash several years back; she did her best to put it from her mind.

The train jostled again.

"That's it! I'm pulling the lever."

"Don't!" said Mr. Foster with haste. "I mean, look at you! You're doing rather well!"

She gave a sorry little nod. If only she had her sister to hug.

"Come now." He stood.

"Where?" Autumn wiped some of the tears away.

He didn't answer so she stood out of curiosity, raising her arms in front of her and crouching to maintain her balance as she moved to the aisle.

"This way," he said, "I have a feeling you will like this."

Mr. Foster walked to the end of the car, and Autumn followed while gripping the seats beside her for stability.

"My word!" shrieked an old lady when Autumn squeezed her hand by mistake.

"Oh, I am ever so sorry!" She stumbled after Mr. Foster, glancing back at the woman in regret.

They went on through several cars. A dining car, a library, and even a lounge. When they got to the car after that, Autumn found a neat little staircase leading upward.

"I didn't know there was a second floor!"

Wind thundered from above.

"You still with me?" Mr. Foster set his hands on the railing and made the climb.

"Yes, yes I'm here."

Mr. Foster pushed open the latch on the roof to reveal the sky. Several large gusts of wind swept across Autumn's hair as she set a foot on the steps.

Autumn gripped the railings and took another step. "What are you doing?"

He said nothing so she climbed higher, nearing the middle of the staircase.

"Take my hand," he ordered.

She obeyed, passing him so that her eyes peeped over the roof of the train as wind roared in her ears and the light blinded her vision. She blinked hard, squinting as the landscape disappeared behind them. She tried in a frantic struggle to go back down but Mr. Foster blocked her way. "Go on," he insisted.

"No! This is too dangerous!" she cried, taking two more steps up, her torso above the hatch. She slowly turned around, taking great care not to stumble.

Mr. Foster climbed higher, forcing Autumn farther.

"Let go!" She yanked her hand from his grasp. She now stood on the second to last step so most of her body was out of the train car with Mr. Foster's head lining up with her chest.

"Ah! Oh! Dear goodness me!" She flung her arms out in attempts at grasping anything and succeed in smacking his face.

"It's okay! Trust me!"

Autumn ceased her struggling and focused on Mr. Foster's unseeing eyes, as she blinked rapidly. "But," she said, her voice catching. "I- I don't want to die." Tears burned down her cheeks, and she sniffed, darting her eyes all around the view.

Mr. Foster reached his hand forward and put it on her side, and she lowered her palm over his, shaking all the while.

"Miss Everleigh, I would never, ever put you in a situation where there was any chance you might die."

She nodded with a swallow and braved the final step. The minute she did, she completely lost her balance and threw her hands out, catching hold of Mr. Foster's waist, squeezing him with all the fear she had in her, afraid that if she let go she would go flying out behind the train to be lost forever.

"Calm down," he soothed. "We haven't even got to the best part."

Autumn didn't want to get to the best part. All she wanted was to remain still until the train stopped.

"Look," said Mr. Foster.

Autumn nodded but didn't open her eyes.

"I am going to hold you like this and keep you in place." He demonstrated by putting one hand around her lower torso. She thought she heard him say something more but couldn't quite hear above the wind.

"Okay," she agreed. She didn't let go.

Mr. Foster's other hand dropped to her waist and tightened. "You can let go of me now. Don't worry; I've got you."

Autumn now had a choice. Cower like a wounded child or face her fears. Cowering certainly sounded more appealing, but there would be no reward.

So, Autumn lifted a shaky hand off his shoulder and opened her eyes as slowly as one waking up on a Sunday morning. She blinked several times to refocus her vision.

Straight ahead, the other train cars shifted back and forth among each other, clattering and thudding across the tracks. Far beyond them, the engine itself billowed a cloud of smoke across the tall mountains on either side of the way where the rocky tips were cloaked in pure white snow.

"Oh! Oh, Mr. Foster! The mountains!" She wiped a loose strand of hair from her face, cracking a smile.

"I know!"

"I could almost touch them!"

The train jostled, and she tipped forward, gripping Mr. Foster's shoulders.

"It's quite all right; you're perfectly safe." He continued to hold her firmly at her waist. Autumn nodded and readjusted herself, sucking in a long breath. She gave a defining exhale and let go of him, squeezing her hands into fists, pressing her elbows to her side.

"Woo!" She erupted into giggles as the wind whipped around her.

What bliss! She was a star! The queen of England herself! No, the world! How silly she had once been to be afraid! Besides, she had full control, didn't she? Did she? No, no she didn't.

Autumn examined Mr. Foster's strong hands around her waist. She wasn't in control at all. He was...

The pretty view caught her attention again, and the whistle blew as the engine neared a tall bridge.

Autumn gave a rosy smile, letting go of all the tension inside her as she thrust both her arms out wide in elation.

The train proceeded across the bridge, revealing a dancing stream reflecting the golden sunlight.

Autumn giggled and gasped to see Mr. Foster laughing too!

They went on, smiling and enjoying the breeze and, for Autumn especially, the sun! Such a pretty way it hit the gorgeous mountains... like how her sister's light shone on herself.

The train eventually chugged into the Carlisle station, slowing to a stop as the first few flakes of snow drifted their way down from the heavens.

"The way the air hit my face!" Autumn shrieked with happiness as they left the train. "It brought me joy just seeing you smiling!"

"And hearing you laughing!"

Autumn did a twirl and gave one last joyous glance at the train. "That was the most extraordinary thing I've ever done!"

"I'm so proud of you!" said Mr. Foster, skipping along, leaving the station.

"Oh, please, it's nothing once you actually start. I was hardly scared a bit!" She bounced beside him and laughed again. "Put out your tongue. Whoever catches a snowflake first, wins!" She hurried forward and stuck out her own tongue.

"I got one!" he boasted.

"Me too!"

How wonderful, indeed! She had actually ridden a train, and enjoyed herself. Autumn raised her focus to Mr. Foster and smiled shyly. She really did have him to thank for everything.

"So," she purposely bumped his arm while brushing her hair to the back of her neck.

"So?"

"What do you think of it all?"

"All of what?"

"Life!"

"Well, I think that it is too short to let it go by so fast."

"I agree!"

They made their way through the falling snow back to the Raven's Nest and soon found themselves standing outside the front of the home alone and under the falling snow.

"I look forward to seeing you again soon," Autumn sighed, not wanting to leave.

"Yes, I must say I agree." He folded his arms and turned his head away.

"I won't be able to come to check on your progress with the stamp for a few days since I am going to A *Christmas Carol* with Patience this week after all. So, here is the envelope with the seal. I trust you to do the job on your own."

He accepted the paper from her, smiling.

"Well?" She tapped her foot with impatience.

"I am listening."

"Are you going to invite me to dance with you at the Winter Ball next week or aren't you?"

"I thought dancing wasn't all that much fun?"

Autumn stepped closer to him, and boldly took his hand "It truly isn't all that bad. Besides, you need the experience to write about it, don't you?"

He laughed. "I guess it would be rude of me to refuse."

"Quite." She neared him, closing her eyes, insides churning. The two inched closer together in their goodbye. Mr. Foster lifted a hand to her shoulder and drew near. As she gazed into his face, Autumn felt dizzy. She thought, for a moment, he might put his lips to her cheek.

"I—" she whispered.

"Yes?"

Autumns eyebrows knitted together as she lowered her gaze to the ground. "I have to go."

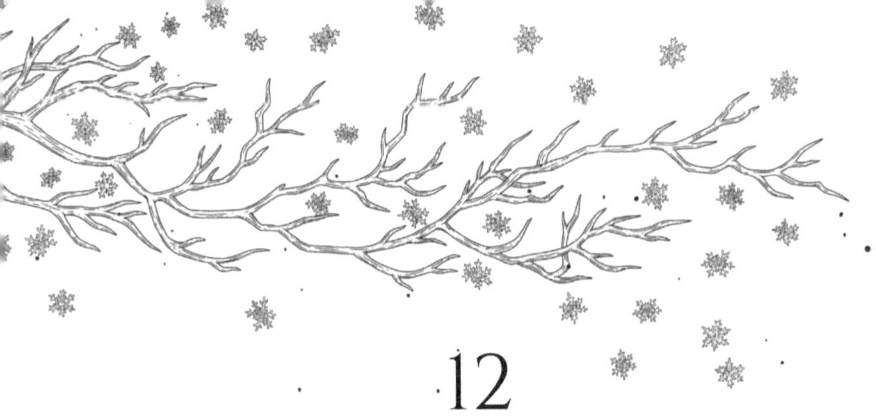

12

To think I might have fallen for him would be preposterous! More than foolish! Utterly absurd, thought Autumn some days later. It was perhaps the hundredth time she'd had the thought.

She continued to silently scold herself as she rummaged through the items spilled across her bed.

I mean, what was I thinking? Just imagine! He and I, in love! Ridiculous. Mr. Foster was no different than all the other men out there: selfish and inconsiderate and entirely unreliable. And yet, Autumn couldn't imagine him ever hurting anyone. In truth, in some ways, he was quite unlike any man she had ever known. Perhaps a life with him would be different to what she had imagined. She shouldn't have left when she had, she should have—

No! She must remind herself that whatever she might be feeling at this present moment in time was temporary. Love was real, of course it was, but so was deception and abandonment. She had been a fool to suggest they attend the ball together.

Autumn forced herself to put a hold on these thoughts; the carriage would arrive at any moment to take her and her sister to the theatre, and she could not be late.

"Handkerchief, money, chocolate," she said, stuffing the items into the bag. She was ready. Almost. Her eyes drifted to her mother's old scrapbook on the chiffonier. She lifted it and flipped through the pages. The formerly blank pages were now stuffed to the brim with memories. Autumn had stayed up most of the night filling the book. It contained their whole life together: bits of poetry Patience had written to her, pressed flowers from a trip to Selten Field, photographs, drawings, the owl feather from their game of chase. There were many more items, each recalling a specific happy moment in the sisters' lives together.

To fill additional pages, Autumn had written down their fondest moments in story form, such as the day with the gingerbread, the night when they mistook the shadow of a cat to be a person, and the time they read their favourite book together in the park on a summer afternoon after they played croquet. As for the last ten or so pages, Autumn had purposefully left those blank.

"Now I am ready." She tucked the book under her arm and stepped in front of the mirror. A simple opera cloak, delicately embroidered, ended at her waist and coordinated with her hand muff and winter bonnet. She'd added a sprig of holly to her hat, too.

Her stomach churned with anticipation as she looked at her reflection. A teary-eyed woman stared back.

"You are going to be fine." She spoke so softly her voice came out in barely a whisper. She headed down the stairs.

"Good, you're ready," Autumn said, nodding at Patience, who wore a white dress, blue opera cloak, and a white faux-fur hand warmer, which Autumn had given her last Christmas.

"Patience your hair is all down in the wrong places." Autumn set the book to the side.

"I'll go fix it." Her sister started to leave the room.

"No, we haven't the time, just let me—" Autumn leaned forward and tucked the naughty strands of blonde hair back into place.

Patience sucked in her breath, causing her chest to rise and fall upon release.

"Almost—" Autumn slid another hair to the side, poking her sister in the ear accidentally.

"Ow!" Patience lunged back, clapping her palm to her sore ear.

"Oh, sorry!" Autumn reached out to her sister. "Are you all right?" She squinted.

"Fine, fine," Patience said, rubbing her ear where it smarted.

Autumn placed both hands on her sister's cheeks as the two locked eyes. They swallowed, staring for a few seconds, before Autumn dropped her hands to her side awkwardly and looked the other way, tucking away her own loose lock of hair into place.

Patience cleared her throat and looked at the floor.

"I have something for you." Autumn picked up the book with haste and hurried beside her sister, placing it in her hands and turning back the cover. "I know I suggested that you fill this with the memories still to come of life in our new home, but I now realise that we have already made so many wonderful memories together…" She let go, watching as her sister turned one page after another, eyes fixed on the book. Patience's eyes filled with tears as she looked.

Autumn reached up and wiped the moisture from her sister's lashes and flipped to the last few pages.

"Patience," Autumn whispered. "These memories don't have to end. We can still make more of them, starting tonight. And tomorrow and the day after that…" she stepped back, waiting for an answer.

Patience flipped back to an earlier page, apparently reading some of the writing. "I—" she whispered, glancing at Autumn.

A horse whinnied outside.

Autumn eyed the window, taking a deep breath. "That's our carriage."

Patience nodded and closed the book, then set it to the side and clasped her handbag with both hands.

A winter wonderland greeted them. Much to Autumn's delight, the entire view consisted of sparkling, unturned snow. The perfect kind for building snowmen in.

Giving a little wave to the carriage driver, she wandered over to one of the thick oak trees in the front yard. She lifted her hand to the crystallised branch and stood on tiptoe to break off a single icicle, letting her breath come out in visible wisps as she turned the icicle over, running a finger up and lightly touching the sharp point. *Perfect. So natural. So mysterious. Just after a fresh snowfall, everything sure seems so perfect, so clean… so right.*

"It's beautiful, isn't it?" she said, turning to Patience.

Her sister nodded. Her eyes were still teary. "We don't want to be late. Come on."

After the driver helped them into the enclosed carriage, into seats facing one another, they were off to the theatre in silence. Neither sibling spoke as they went through the bumpy, uneven snow, the carriage bouncing every time they hit a drift.

Time went by, and still not a word passed between them as Autumn stared sadly with her face pressed against the window, watching rosy-faced children in the town with their hands in the air trying to catch the falling snow on their pink tongues. She almost wished she could join them. They seemed so happy together, making snow angels and having snowball fights, laughing and giggling with one another. Autumn and Patience had done all those things just last year. Everything was different, now.

She turned her head a little and peeked at Patience. Her sister must have been attempting the same feat for the two women locked eyes, frowned, and looked away again quickly.

"Well," said Patience, folding her arms.

Autumn said nothing.

"The least we can do is enjoy each other's company." Patience faced her sister once more.

"Did you want to apologise first?" Autumn asked.

"I don't hear you apologising to me." Patience glanced back at the window. "It's certainly a nice snowfall."

"Yes, it certainly is," said Autumn with little effort.

"Do you remember when we built that snow fort last year, and you accidentally threw a snowball right into old Mr. Grumpy's back?"

"Yes," a smile threatened to form on her lips. "And then you threw one at Lady Lizzy at the same time!"

"And they both turned around and blamed one another!" said Patience with a giggle, and both girls laughed until their eyes met again and Patience gave a little cough.

"Your dress looks lovely," Autumn said, pulling at the tip of her pointer finger.

"Thank you."

Autumn hugged herself.

Patience put her face against the window and mumbled a light tune under her breath,

"Hum ditty, hum ditty, off in a daydream,

Won't you come and dance with me?

Hum ditty, hum ditty, off in a daydream,

Won't you come and dance with me?"

Her soft voice echoed with vibrance within the small cabin. Autumn looked at her sister with wide eyes, opening her mouth to sing the next line,

"Hey oh, the whirlwind blows

Through the highs and through the lows.

Hey oh, the whirlwind blows

And sweeps us 'til the sun comes down."

Patience continued, and both sisters joined in unison:

"We are jolly in the morning light,

Till the dawn, and all seems right.

You and me, we wiggle our toes.

It's us together in the wind and snows.

Hey oh, the whirlwind blows
Through the highs and through the lows.
Hey oh, the whirlwind blows
And sweeps us 'til the sun comes down.
It's me and you to the end of time,
When in the dark and in our prime,
We hold each other through thick and thin.
I'll love you through your greatest sin!
Hey oh, the whirlwind blows
Through the highs and through the lows.
Hey oh, the whirlwind blows
And sweeps us till the sun comes down.
Hum ditty, hum ditty, off in a daydream,
Won't you come and dance with me?
Hum ditty, hum ditty, off in a daydream,
Thank you for the dance with me..."

The sisters finished and Patience cupped her hands together, smiling with closed lips.

"How do you remember that song?" Autumn said, clutching her chest, eyes a tad watery.

"I don't know." Patience shook her head. "I heard it someplace before, though I'm sure it must have been years ago."

Autumn nodded solemnly.

"I used to sing it to you, when you were very little. Whenever you were upset or scared, I would sing a few lines, and you would always join in before too long. Or sometimes you would start, and I'd follow."

Patience gave a small smile. Autumn smiled back.

"I miss those days."

"Me too."

They looked away, and Autumn crossed her arms, but that didn't last more than two seconds before she sighed and let them drop.

"I can't bear it any longer. If we are going to be together, we might as well have some fun."

"Really! I mean, yes. I agree," Patience said while twiddling her fingers. "But this doesn't mean we're on good terms or anything." She raised one brow.

"Oh, definitely not." Autumn folded her hands in her lap while biting her bottom lip. "I'm still just as angry with you as you are with me."

"Of course."

"Quite."

Both nodded.

"So... a temporary truce?" Patience held out a hand.

"Truce." Autumn reached forward and shook it. She was ever so tempted to hug her sister in that moment but felt that would be just a bit too much.

"Look!" Patience squealed and smacked her on the knee.

There, in all its glory, sat the theatre.

As soon as the carriage came to a halt, Patience took her sister by the hand and ran for the theatre. Autumn gathered their things with her free hand and thanked the driver as Patience dragged her away.

"It always seems grander than I remember it. Every time."

Autumn's foot sank into a little drift of snow; she would have landed flat on her nose had Patience not caught her.

As they neared the building, they found the front steps of the theatre flooded with people wearing evening clothes, some made from the finest silk, some adorned with animal fur. Conversations were gay as couples and families approached the doors.

The peppermint fragrance of Christmas mixed with pine and mistletoe was thick in the air.

The sisters entered the doors, admiring the thick garland strung over the arches as they felt the warmth inside surround them.

"Look!" Patience pointed to a violin player in one corner of the stuffy lobby and dashed over with Autumn stumbling along. She let go of her sister and clapped to the beat of the music, tipping her head side to side.

"Autty, how fun this is!"

Autumn smiled to hear her sister say her name.

The musician finished the number, and the sisters clapped and cheered louder than anyone else around them, drawing quite the stare.

"The cocoa!" Autumn said, heading for the nearby concession stand with a bounce in her step.

"You two look lovely this evening," said the cashier with a glowing smile. "How might I assist you?"

"Two hot cocoas and a buttered popcorn please!" Autumn faced Patience. "And a candied popcorn for you right, Pay-pay?"

Patience's face lit up, and she gave a nod.

After they received the refreshments, they strolled toward their seats. Patience munched on her popcorn all the way there.

"Shall we get some opera glasses?" asked Autumn, stopping at a stall.

"Oh, yes!"

Autumn selected a pair and paid for them before heading to find their seats.

"Names and tickets," an employee said, holding out his hand and preventing them from leaving the lobby.

"Patience and Autumn Everleigh." Autumn tried balancing her food and drink under her chin while reaching for her handbag. "Would you hold these?" she asked Patience, who obliged.

The man accepted the tickets, pointed to his clipboard, and said, "The left-hand box, on the third floor."

Autumn tilted her head. "Oh, I think there might be a mistake... I purchased tickets in row ten. We don't have a box."

He pointed to his clipboard. "Says here that you have been upgraded to a box. It's that way," he pointed over his shoulder and looked past the women to the next patron.

"Patience!" Autumn whispered, a pulse of energy rushing through her chest as they entered the hall leading to the theatre. "We're sitting in a box!"

"But... how? Don't they cost about ten times as much as regular seats? Do you think it's a mistake?" she was whispering, too, in case someone realised the mix up and sent them the other way.

It must have been Mr. Foster... he's the only one who knew anything about the trip to the theatre, wasn't he?

Autumn smiled at Patience, but paused before she could share her theory.

The man was certainly kind enough to think of such a thing, but he could never afford such an expensive luxury. No, it must be something else.

Patience jabbed her sister in the arm. "Solving the mystery?"

"Oh, I don't know," Autumn said, her voice coming out in a faded whisper, for at that moment they rounded the corner to behold the stage itself, shimmering in all her prestigious glory. The carved wooden frame was tall and handsome, housing the closed blood-red curtains with golden tassels swaying lightly over the stage.

Vibrant gold detail captured Autumn's attention as she was taken in by the magnificence of the room. The shimmering walls flickered beneath the crystal chandeliers above seats packed together in dozens of rows. A variety of sounds reached their ears, as other attendees chattered and argued while finding their places in the midst of the chaos. Far away, near the base of the stage, the band rehearsed their numbers, tuning instruments and flipping through music sheets, while the conductor himself polished his glossy baton.

"Come, quickly. Before they change their minds!" Autumn pulled her sister along, giggling with delight.

The sisters lost their way more than once before they finally found their seats. They sat, feeling rather flustered from the havoc of getting there.

"Of course," as Patience put it now, "it truly wasn't his *fault*. After all, the dear soul really thought he was helping..."

The 'dear soul' in questions was a somewhat irate and very, very elderly man who had given the sisters strict directions to their box after enquiring, very loudly, where they were heading. Autumn did her best to move past him, but Patience explained their dilemma. He spoke with the authority of a headmaster and with the volume of someone rather deaf,

"Now, see here young lady, you must head to the stage and take a right. That will lead you to the correct set of stairs!"

Autumn got into an awful dispute with him and argued until Patience pulled her away. They ended up trying his recommended route out of politeness which, of course, turned out to be incorrect. They had to walk all the way across the aisle yet again, apologising for knocking over drinks and treats more than twice. After stepping quite hard on a very annoyed woman's new shoes, Autumn had been so upset that she even tried to find the old man to give him a piece of her mind, but she failed to relocate the fellow.

"It is kind of funny, though," Patience laughed now as they sat together in their private box.

"Yes, I suppose it is. Besides, we have our seats now, and that is what counts!"

"Oh, look!" Patience pulled her sister's arm and peered over the railing of the two-seater box.

What a view they had indeed! They could see everything! All the band players, the lights, and the entirety of the stage. And if Autumn only stretched her neck like so—yes! She could just make out the entire audience.

"The people in the back are so tiny! Like little toys."

"This is even better than I ever imagined!" Autumn clapped with delight.

Patience leaned back, pulled out her bag of popcorn and munched on the last of the sugary pieces.

"What ever happened to saving some for the show?" Autumn scolded with a smile and shake of the head.

"Too tempting!" Patience said and only half swallowed one of the pieces. She erupted into a fit of coughing. "Hot cocoa, hot cocoa," she gasped as Autumn rushed to hand her sister the beverage.

Patience quickly took the drink, held it to her mouth, and chugged. "Oh!" She gave another nasty cough.

"All right?"

"Fine, fine." Patience made a fist and gave her diaphragm a good hard whack. At that moment the lights dimmed, and she screamed in a raspy voice, "It's starting!"

"Shush!" Autumn leaned closer to her sister, eyes lit with wonder and locked on the stage.

Bong... bong... bong... bong... bong... bong... A clock bell rang as the curtains opened and a spotlight revealed a single figure carrying a torch.

Footsteps echoed throughout the theatre as more people emerged on stage, carrying a coffin.

The first man took out a pipe, gave a puff, and spoke.

"Marley was dead, to begin with, there was no doubt whatsoever about that..."

The scene flourished with light as carolers appeared, singing softly. Their voices grew louder and louder until a hunched over, wrinkled old man emerged in the centre of them all.

"Scrooge!" Patience cupped her hands together.

"I know!" said Autumn. She clutched her sibling as if witnessing an intense moment frozen in time.

The music picked up as Scrooge began his daily routine, heading though the snowy streets of town to work.

Autumn closed her eyes and felt the music. It was beautiful; melodic and sweet. She wished she could listen to an orchestra every day as the notes rose and fell.

The carolers on the scene were as lighthearted and joyous as Christmas itself, just as Autumn felt in this very moment as she clung to her sister.

Scrooge was soon confronted by his old coworker Marley, who warned him of the spirits yet to come. The sisters gasped so loud everyone on stage must have heard them, for they were sure that Scrooge himself winked at Patience!

The longer the show went on, the more her sister gave little yawns, tipping her head close to Autumn but always pulling it back. However, now, as her eyelids drooped, she slowly placed her head on her sister's shoulder.

Autumn's eyes welled up with tears as she lowered her head atop Patience's in return. She found her sister's fingers in the darkness and intertwined their hands as they watched Scrooge revisit memories of his youth.

Autumn even noticed Patience quiver a few tears and couldn't help wondering if it was because of Tiny Tim or the fact that they were together again and at peace for once. Either way she did not ask, for the night was too perfect: hand in hand with her sister, their differences forgotten entirely, at least for the moment. Both were calm and relaxed like old times, eating the last of the popcorn, sipping away at the luscious hot cocoa, and watching the most wonderful performance in the world.

The play soon ended, and both cried a little, wishing it could have gone on forever.

They shivered in the snow outside but soon found their carriage and were headed home together once more.

Just moments before dozing off, Patience pulled Autumn's cloak tighter around her shoulders. Her eyelids hovered open as the carriage wheels ground through battered snow.

"Autumn?" she whispered, eyes drooping.

"Yes, Patience?"

"I love you..."

Autumn squeezed her lids shut and hugged her sister. "I love you, too." As she closed her eyes, she could hardly believe they had ever fought at all. It seemed so unlikely now. If she had felt anger before, she certainly didn't now. All she felt was a gentle peace that she fervently wished would go on forever.

13

"I am confused," Autumn said to Mrs. Glendale, accepting the small box she offered.

"Mr. Foster asked me to give it to you," answered she. Her face was very red.

Autumn lowered her eyes to the gift and lifted one corner to peek in. Her stamp! Mr. Foster had finished!

"Oh, oh thank you, Mrs. Glendale!" Her stomach felt full of butter-flies as said her goodbyes and hurried home.

Once Autumn arrived in her bedroom, she struck a match. With trembling fingers, she dripped hot wax onto the envelope of the letter she had written to Patience from 'Mr. Williams.' After a moment, she took the stamp and lowered the tip onto the wet wax. *One... two... three...*

four... five... She removed the stamp, leaving behind a perfect configuration of Mr. Williams' crest. It was done.

"Now what?" Autumn fretted. She tidied her hair, then paced back and forth while everything from the past two weeks fought for attention all at once in her mind

One pleasant evening together and I feel unable to go through with this trick. She felt close to tears. *Is this truly what's best for Patience?*

For several days she privately pondered this very question. She could not bring herself to post the letters, which she now kept hidden in her handbag. Their night at the theatre had reminded Autumn how much she truly adored her sister. She would do anything to protect her—but would posting the letters hurt the girl more? To think that she still wanted to leave her for Mr. Williams hurt Autumn. That selfish, risk-indulgent man! Autumn could not allow Patience to marry him. That was out of the question. Keeping Patience safe was more important than anything. Even if it meant she felt a little pain.

No matter how hard she tried to convince herself that she was in the right, Autumn felt a nagging, pulling in her chest that told her otherwise. She didn't want to break poor Patience's heart; a broken engagement between her and Mr. Williams would surely devastate her.

Autumn loved her sister. She wanted her to be happy. *What if I've been wrong? What if marrying Mr. Williams made Patience feel as happy as I felt at the theatre all the time?* Maybe Mr. Williams could keep Patience safe after all and Autumn could even come to love Mr. Foster.

No! What was she thinking? Mr. Williams was the same man he had always been. He was prideful, self-centred and careless! And Mr. Foster was no better, just another person in her life who might abuse her trust.

"What am I doing?" Autumn said as tears formed, and she cried and cried until her eyes were dry and it was time to get ready for the Winter Ball that evening.

Every year the wealthiest homes of Carlisle took turns sponsoring the party. This year, it was the turn of the parents of Hortense Fontaine. Patience was fond of Hortense and Hortense loved Patience, too. She had been looking forward to the party for a long time, far before Mr. Williams returned from his travels.

When both Autumn and her sister were ready, they walked arm in arm down the snowy street. Despite her conflicting feelings, Autumn looked forward to seeing Mr. Foster again. She wore her finest dress and had applied her favourite lavender perfume. While she never would have admitted it to anyone, she'd added an extra spritz for the sake of Mr. Foster. *If he can't see me, he'll know me by the scent.*

Her gown was the finest she'd ever worn.

"Straight out of a fairytale!" Patience had gushed. It was light pink in colour with an off-the-shoulder bodice, short puffed sleeves, and a generous row of ivory buttons running down the middle of her torso. The overskirt was voluminous and ran to the floor with a modest train. Autumn had rarely felt so grand.

Completing her look were elbow-length white satin gloves and her fan; she'd pulled most of her hair high on top of her head and adorned it with a band of white feathers. Two curled wisps on either side of her face were not quite long enough to touch her shoulders. She'd twirled experimentally before the mirror to ensure it would stay in place if she did indeed decide to dance.

Patience was also a sight to behold, in a sky-blue gown with long sleeves and a low neckline. Her overskirt was tightly fitted around the waist and gradually expanding toward the ruffled hem. Her blonde hair had been brushed into a neat bun.

"I can't get over it." Patience shook her head, a light smile forming as they walked. "You of all people are taking me to a ball! Autumn, has something *happened* to you?"

Autumn giggled. "Oh hush! It cannot be that miserable! It's not like anyone else is going to steal you away now."

Patience didn't answer. Autumn gave her a playful push to show she was teasing but stopped when she saw Patience's face.

"Patty, whatever is the matter?" She tightened her hold on her sister's arm.

"Mr. Williams... He's..."

"He's what, darling?"

Patience cocked her head, leaning close to whisper, "He's not coming."

"Oh but he is! He agreed to show as of last night."

"Yes," her lips quivered. "Though I should have listened to you."

They stopped walking in the middle of the snowy street and faced each other, carriages moving around them.

"Patience, what happened?" Autumn reached forward, wiping the tears from her sister's eyes.

"The press," she choked, "approached him. With the offer of... of an immediate trip to London. To discuss the world tour. I asked if I might accompany him, but he refused. He says he'll be back before Christmas Eve."

Autumn's heart shattered for her sister, while relief flooded her mind at the same time. "Patience. I am so sorry."

"Don't be. I never cared about some silly dancing anyway. I am sure it will all work out in the end. But Autumn, I... I can't help but feel you may have been right about him all along. About everything! He's already forgotten all about me."

Autumn took Patience by the hands. Her internal debate over whether she needed to post the fictitious letters or not may have been solved for her. She knew she should feel happy. But she didn't feel glad at all.

"Well," she said, rubbing her thumb over her sister's hand. "Here's what we'll do. Even if Mr. Williams can't be with us tonight, let us rejoice in having each other, despite his absence, and enjoy the party. We'll worry about his behaviour in the morning. It will all be all right."

Patience nodded, giving a sniffle. "Thank you, Autumn."

They went on, both in better spirits by the time they arrived at the Fontaine estate, which was nothing short of glorious. Rows upon rows of garlands greeted them upon arrival, filled with berries, pine cones, little fruits and mistletoe mingling in the falling snow. Dozens of lanterns lit the front path, cascading flickers of dancing warmth across the arriving guests, some walking and others in carriages leaving wheel trails behind in the snow. The grand home stood beside the grandest pine tree one could imagine, tall and proud, decked with popcorn strings, berries, and little treasures.

Autumn and Patience had barely set foot on the property before they flinched at a sudden high-pitched shriek.

"Je suis choqué!" Hortense flew down the grand front steps three at a time, colliding with everyone in her path, as she embraced the sisters with a big bear hug, her black ringlets bouncing over her shoulders.

"I cannot believe you are both here!" She squealed in her thick French accent, eyes darting between them with a twinkle. "Your hair is so pretty!" She ran her fingers through one of Autumn's strands. "This is going to be the greatest ball you ever did attend! We opened the entirety of the downstairs to everyone. Dining, music, games, dancing! The courtyard is full of drinks and activities—and, of course, more dancing!"

Autumn laughed shyly at the enthusiastic welcome. She was already glad she'd come.

"Come, come!" Hortense linked arms with them both and pulled them inside. As soon as they entered, they were greeted by a flood of people. Hortense and Patience disappeared, leaving Autumn in wide-eyed confusion to mingle with the other guests. She found the cloak room, left her handbag and outdoor wear behind, and ventured into the hall alone, squinting and trying to make her way into some open space to get a drink and see if she could find Mr. Foster; in this stampede, she would be lucky to find her own hand!

People were everywhere, leaning against walls, sitting in chairs, and talking left and right, whispering to loved ones and shouting with friends as they lifted glasses of brandy.

Autumn slid her fingers under her left dress sleeve to ventilate herself a bit, for a sort of dampness lingered in the air, causing things to feel stuffy. She strode on past the dance floor, not able to help but peek in.

The sounds of the music caressed her ears as she watched the happy dancers in the centre of the room.

The dance used eight people separated into two rows with one side male and the other female, each couple holding one end of a scarf, creating a sort of tunnel. The pair at the front of the line would lower their ribbon, the lady winding the fabric around her torso until she reached her partner and proceeded to waltz through the channel, only unwinding when they reached the end, taking their new spots in line and raising the scarf so the new pair could have a turn dancing through.

"Excuse me, miss," a gentleman with long sideburns approached her, followed by another young man, who was a foot or so shorter than Autumn.

She glanced down at him, her mind elsewhere. "I beg your pardon?"

"I present to you, Mr. Brooke," said the first man.

"Oh." Autumn swallowed, her stomach churning as she stepped back. She needed to get some fresh air. "Can I help you?" She examined both of them, not having seen either before in all her life.

"May I have the honour of dancing this set with you?" said Mr. Brooke, bowing.

A choke caught hold of her throat as her heart wrenched from her chest and into her mouth. "N-n-no, thank you. I am taken—" And she stumbled away, putting a hand over her mouth to prevent throwing up as she left a red-faced Mr. Brooke behind.

Autumn found the nearest door, shoved past the guests, and let herself out into the cool evening air.

She inhaled, letting the breeze liberate her soul. A softer sensation of sounds took hold of her as she stood on an open balcony overlooking the courtyard. The vivid scene could have easily been mistaken for Christmas day itself, decked with a calm gayety of couples and green pine trees with candles decorating the cobblestone path and guiding partners through a winter wonderland of love.

"How exquisite!" said Patience, sitting beside a fountain below as she took hold of Hortense's arm and laughed. Autumn couldn't help smiling at her happy sister.

"Autty!" Patience waved up at her, voice level far above proper etiquette. "You left us!"

Autumn let her face slip into joy as she slid her fan strap over her wrist and went down to join her sister.

"You simply must tell her of your home in France," said Patience to her friend, cupping her hands together.

Hortense opened her lips in the biggest of smiles while pulling on one of her curls. "Indeed, for we have been most blessed with great farmlands of seventy acres and horses! *Père* says I am rather spoiled."

"Will you go riding on your trip next month?" asked Patience.

Hortense shook her head. "I meant to tell you. I delayed my travels due to the conditions of my mother. She is ill, and I wish to remain by her side until her restoration."

"But this means so much to you! You have been waiting to return to France for years. To see your cousins and grandparents!"

"And I will have another chance in the autumn. I don't mind. I would rather spend these days with *Maman* than leave her for my own enjoyment."

Autumn couldn't help glancing at Patience at this, the two locking eyes.

"Ah, look here," Hortense took the sisters by the shoulders and ducked behind them, grip slipping. "It's Mr. Lawrence!"

"Hello, young ladies," said he, approaching them.

Hortense's cheeks burned as she stood upright. She squeezed her lids shut and then stepped out from behind the shadows of the sisters. "How wonderful to be in your presence again, *monsieur*," she said, eyes darting all around his figure.

"And to be in yours, beautiful Miss Hortense Fontaine. And the company of Hortense, who are also quite fair and ever so beautiful." He swept his arm to his stomach and bowed, putting his head near the floor so that his curly hair flipped over his eyes. He stood, nodding at Autumn. "Pleasant to speak with you as always, Miss Everleigh."

"The pleasure is all mine. Forgive me for being... ill-mannered when last we spoke.

"I recall no such indiscretion. You have never been anything but extremely pleasant."

"Did Mr. Foster tell you of my visit to the Ivory?"

"He did and mentioned you much of the evening. You enjoyed your time, I hope?"

"Oh, yes. I have never seen a more breathtaking home."

He nodded, facing Hortense, whose face grew scarlet. "I was going to ask—"

"*Oui!*" Hortense gave a jump. "My answer is yes! When is the wedding? How many children do you want? I was thinking twelve, perhaps thirteen? *Tu es une personne merveilleux!*"

He raised a quizzical brow. "My question was, would you honour me with your hand for the next quadrille—and as many more as you'd like thereafter?"

Hortense's pupils expanded as the tips of her ears seethed with red. She opened her mouth, but nothing came out, and gave a vigorous nod instead of words.

"Their relationship is off to a great start," Patience said after the couple disappeared inside.

"Oh, yes, so long as Hortense can stand the wait for the actual proposal."

Both sisters chuckled. What a night indeed. Autumn glanced around at the pretty little picture decked with reds and greens, shimmering candles, and happy people. And she was one of them!

Her gaze shifted to the balcony. Mr. Williams stood at the top, then began his descent, skipping most of the steps as he approached the sisters. He wore a tight black suit and polka-dot green cravat around his neck. "Miss Everleigh, Miss Patience Everleigh," he whispered. He looked very serious.

"What are you doing here?" asked Patience, face sullen. "Shouldn't you be in London?"

Mr. Williams shook his head, dropping to one knee. "No. I should not be in London. My place is here, with you. I cancelled the trip."

"Cancelled?" the sisters said in unison.

"Yes. I came here to repent and beg your forgiveness, though I am certainly not worthy of reconciliation. I was a fool to abandon you in your sorrow for the sole reason of self-promotion, which I regret to inform you was consciously done. I didn't realise my sins until I arrived at the station, and I left before boarding to make it back on time."

"Did you run all the way here in the cold?" asked Patience, feeling his damp sleeve.

"All the way, for you mean more to me than any business or travel ever could, and I swear to put the health of our relationship at the forefront of all else, if you will ever manage to forgive me?"

Autumn watched Patience from the corner of her eye.

Patience fanned her face with one hand and let out a teary laugh, falling into his arms. "Of course, I can forgive you!"

Autumn cried too, though far more discreetly. Her face burned, not with cold but with shame.

She had misjudged Mr. Williams. Misjudged him terribly. He really did have a lasting love for Patience. He was willing to throw away all his success for her. He was not the person Autumn had thought him to be; rather, he was the person who Patience had hoped him to be. He was a man who desired to keep his wife happy and safe above all else, which meant that if she separated the pair now, the heartbreak would be beyond compare.

Autumn wiped her eyes and left quietly, leaving them to their joyful reconciliation. She went back inside and roamed the crowded halls once more, attempting to distract herself from her thoughts by looking at the pretty details of the Christmas decorations inside and searching for Mr. Foster. Where was he, anyway? Would he even show? If he did, she would have to dance...

A chill took hold of her arms and shocked her whole body. She should never have committed to such a thing! Maybe he would forget all about her promise to dance and the two of them could just sit and talk outside. No. She had made a promise, and she couldn't break it. She would ready herself, just in case, by observing the dancers awhile.

Autumn strode down a hall, eyes fixed on the ceiling as she headed into the next room and with an "Oh!" she tripped into the giddy ring of dancers. The music thundered at two-four time, catching her off guard, as a blonde-haired man took her hand, placed his other around the waist and whisked her into the galop!

She attempted to pull away but couldn't and was forced across the ballroom with quick steps, hopping along at an embarrassing rate compared to that of her partner.

The man stepped, took a hop, kicked one leg to the side, and clicked both feet together, repeating and chasséing to the left as Autumn's cheeks seethed with colour. She attempted to follow along, always managing to jump a second too late and clicking her shoes in a way that when she hit the floor, she lost her balance and clenched her partner's hand much too tightly.

Out flew his right leg, then the left as she attempted to follow, not able to keep up, no matter how hard she tried.

"Oh goodness!" Autumn whispered, closing her eyes as her adrenaline rushed. If only she could slow things down a little! Take a minute to gather her breath. This was all so sudden!

She blinked her eyes open with a gasp as the happy-go-lucky face of her fellow dancer faded away. In its place emerged the image of her late father, smiling down at his twelve-year-old girl once more. The music and talking of the party guests colliding with each other faded into the distant sound of someone humming a tune in her thoughts.

"And back and forth, back and forth," the voice of her father echoed as he led the swift dance motions while holding on to his daughter.

"Oh, Papa, I love dancing!"

Autumn tried to blink the memory away, but the picture of her father remained, this time saying,

"You are the greatest dancer of all time! I promise I will always be there to provide for you and your sister. Always..."

"Liar!" Autumn gritted her teeth and blinked at the tears streaming her face. This was a mistake! She should have never come to this ball in the first place. She had to stop dancing, now.

"What is wrong, my dewdrop?"

"Stop. Talking. To. Me," she hissed

"You sound upset."

"Because you left me!"

"I would never leave you."

"Enough!"

Her father's imaginary face subsided into a blurry view, disappearing, as in its place blossomed the very real image of her dance partner, who smiled and continued leading her in the galop.

Autumn exhaled as she left the reverie. She didn't know if it was luck, a fairy godmother, or a source unknown, but her mind gave way to peace as she found herself spinning around with a smile forming and tears of relief washing her neck.

She kicked to the side, this time in sync with her partner as they did a half turn, her painful memories drifting away.

The jolly dance soon came to a close, the orchestra ending in a triumphant note of conclusion as Autumn curtsied to her partner, thanking him amid her bliss before wandering to the sidelines, thoughts in the clouds.

She placed a hand across her heaving chest, dipping forward and laughing to herself. She had danced. Actually danced! And no one was going to stop her from doing it again.

Autumn slid the fan off her wrist, flipping it open in modesty to hide her burning face, eyes taking in the merry sights of the room. Through the doors to the ballroom entered Mr. Foster, who walked near the pianist, squinting and cocking his head as if listening for a sense of direction.

She headed over to him, giggling in pleasure. "Mr. Foster!"

"Miss Everleigh."

"I am ever so pleased at your arrival!" Autumn exclaimed, noticing his black tailcoat, white gloves, vest, and bow tie.

"And I of yours," he said, as a smile lit his face.

The orchestra signaled the start of a waltz, and the crowd lowered their conversation, once more drifting to the dance floor. All became still save for the soft music.

"Shall we begin?" Autumn raised a dainty left hand to Mr. Foster's shoulder and placed the other in his palm. He said nothing, only connected his fingers to her waist as they took a few steps backward to reserve space in the ring.

The violin harmonised, and they started to spin in correspondence with the crowd, using quick steps and extending their clasped hands to head level with the airy notes directing their every flow of movement.

They danced in circles, then took a few steps, and let go of each other's hand, walking side by side, as Autumn's left arm gestured gracefully and Mr. Foster pressed his knuckles to his back. The couple turned into each other again, and he retook her hand, both proceeding with a few steps and repeating, letting go of the other's hand, walking side by side, and coming face to face once more.

Autumn squinted, focusing on his face. If only his eyes could meet hers, but she could feel his emotion all the same. "Mr. Foster, I thought you said you never had danced. Look at you; you're a natural!"

He laughed, "I said I hadn't danced in years. Quite a different thing."

"Quite indeed! You move with the grace of an angel!"

His brows furrowed. "Clarinda used to say that."

"I beg your pardon?"

"My fiancée."

"Your..." they slowed to a stop. Autumn rested her hands on his shoulders, ready to cry. "Mr. Foster, are you engaged?" Her shock was clear in her voice. Fiancée? Had he abandoned her? No! It couldn't be true!

"Please, I am not engaged. I was, but it was more than ten years ago now. Clarinda was my fiancée and she was also the first to abandon me after..." He gestured vaguely towards his eyes.

"I am so sorry. I had no idea," she choked, pulling away only for him to take her hand again.

"Don't be. I saw who she really was once I inherited my uncle's riches. She returned a second and last time, but not for my heart. She is the one to whom I gave my fortune."

Autumn blinked, crying in relief. "You, too, know what it's like to lose someone you love."

"To suffer under your own faults is the penalty of a fool, but to suffer under the choice of the wicked is punishment underserved."

She reached down, lifted his hand, and kissed the surface before intertwining their fingers. "I would... I could never abandon someone I loved for selfish pleasure."

"No, I don't believe you could."

Autumn smiled. Mr. Foster was a wonderful person, and dancing really was the most wonderful and extraordinary feeling in the whole, entire world.

She let her eyes take in the rest of the room, catching the sight of another couple waltzing together, chatting in whispers, and giving long drawn-out blinks. Come to think of it, nearly everyone in the room was dancing and talking quietly, as if in their own worlds with their partners.

"So, tell me," she said, making her voice lighter than usual. "Were you always as good at dressing up as you are at dancing?"

"I dare say yes," answered he. "I'd ask the same of you if I knew your outfit."

"Pink," Autumn said, with a smile. "With golden detail."

He led her in a twirl, letting go so that, when she faced him again, she lifted her hands and rested the gloves on her dress, bending her knees in a curtsey, hem sinking into the floor, as Mr. Foster swept his hands back and drew them in front, offering his open palms. She accepted with grace, and both proceeded to shimmy to the left.

"I shall ask you another question, if I may?" said she.

"Of course."

"What did you look like as a child?" Autumn placed her hand on his shoulder as he took her waist again.

"Small. Bony, with pale skin, short hair, and a face full of curiosity. Young me liked hands-on activities like crafting, as well as reading."

"I should have liked to meet him."

Mr. Foster nodded. "And what did you look like as a child?"

"Oh, I don't know." Autumn shook her head, biting her lip. "Innocent for a small time with short hair, a bit lighter than it is now. Little me always wore the fanciest dress she could get her hands on and loved to bake, as I do now. She was neat and clean and liked to play with her sister."

Mr. Foster remained silent and turned his head away, swallowing. Autumn wondered what was wrong. Still he said nothing, while keeping his face aimed at the ground as they went on with the waltz. She opened her mouth to speak but thought better of it.

"Miss Everleigh," he said, lifting his head and speaking with such a low tone that she thought he might be upset. "What do you look like now?"

Autumn's pupils expanded to double the size as her jaw fell. Why, poor Mr. Foster! To think, after all they had been through together, he didn't even know what she looked like!

"Why, I... I am about five foot four, and have large, dark hazel eyes that have seen so, so very much. Too much, perhaps. Under that follows my nose, small and triangular with a round tip. I have a thin upper lip married to the thicker lower one. And then of course my hair... a mix of dark and light brown."

"May I see you?"

"Of course."

His breath stopped as he took his hand off her side, hesitating as he lifted his palm to her face, running his fingers over her nose and forehead, chin and cheeks causing the butterflies in her to soar. He went on, stroking her closed eyes and lips.

"And how might you wear your hair this evening?"

"One couldn't be too sure." Autumn held her breath.

He brushed his fingers over her forehead and touched her hair lightly, so as not to dishevel it.

"Up, high up. With... feathers?"

"Yes," Autumn laughed and so did he. They danced in silence, as she inched closer to him with every movement, not wanting the night to end.

The rest of the evening was wonderful. They chatted and went outside for fresh air once in a while but always came back in to dance under the holly, for Autumn said she loved that most.

"I must ask," she said later, when they stood on the balcony overlooking the falling snow. "Now that you've experienced *proper* dancing, how might you describe it?"

"As nothing less than the most wonderful and extraordinary feeling in the whole entire world."

Autumn blushed as the wind played with her hair in the dazzling moonlight and wished that things could go on like this forever.

Later, when Mr. Foster went to find them some water, Autumn waited for his return in one of the many open rooms, this one with a few chairs and a young girl showing off her pianoforte skills for a mild audience.

Autumn couldn't help but stand in the corner and laugh to herself. She had been so wrong. Wrong about everything; Mr. Foster, Mr. Williams, Patience. Suddenly, she could see no reason why life couldn't go on as it was now. My, how wonderful it would be to feel this happy every day. Dancing, chatting with Patience, whispering with Mr. Foster. It would be like paradise on earth.

The pianoforte song ended, and in walked Mr. Williams, carrying a plate with blancmange, Patience's favourite.

"Miss Everleigh." He nodded, slowing to a stop when he saw her, his enthusiasm fading.

"Mr. Williams!" She smiled at him for the first time since the proposal. "Are you having a pleasant evening?"

"Most agreeable. Yourself?"

"Very wonderful," she sighed, focusing her gaze on the floor. "Thank you…"

"For what do I deserve the honour of your praise?"

"For coming back for her."

The man's face morphed into an expression of joy as he set the plate down on a table. "Miss Everleigh, I have been a fool."

"And stubborn, too, although I myself am of the same fault."

"On the contrary, I have been the greater fool for attempting to convince you of my love for your sister without changing my actions in accordance. And that is why I came back. I will heretofore put my love for Patience above everything else in my life. From this moment forward, her happiness and safety come first, my business second."

Autumn enclosed his hand between her two gloves and smiled unreservedly.

"Do you believe me now when I say our love will last?"

She blinked back tears. "Yes, yes, I believe I do."

"And I intend to keep my spoken word as I shared previously, for I love your sister, and I promise to always be there for her, no matter what."

Autumn's eyes widened as her father's words came suddenly to mind: 'I promise I will always be there for you and your sister.'

She lifted a hand to her necklace and gripped the ring, pulling so hard the chain snapped, sending beads scattering through the air and hitting the glossy wooden floors.

"Watch out!" Mr. Williams dropped to his knees, hurrying to collect the bouncing ornaments.

Autumn didn't help him. Instead, she squeezed the ring in her hand and stared. Mr. Williams' words rang in her mind, as did her father's.

Their promises were the same. Both lies.

Autumn put her hands one on top of the other over her chest and fled from the room, leaving Mr. Williams and dashing in and out of the baffled partygoers as she ran. In and out she went, sobbing as her father's words laughed in her ears over and over. 'I promise I will always be there... I promise I will always be there... I promise I will always be there...'

She collected her things from the cloak room and fled from the building.

"Pardon me!" she shoved past a few departing guests on the front steps of the house, no longer caring to admire the beautiful decorations of the garden.

Her skirts made running near impossible, though she did her best, lifting her train so the snow wouldn't soak the material.

Puffs of breath wafted from her mouth as she went, nose red and eyeballs on fire when she arrived at the Carlisle post office sometime later.

She stood there in the black of night, staring at the red postbox as if still unsure of what to do, but inside her decision had been made.

Autumn uncurled her fingers one at a time to reveal the ring from her broken necklace.

"Here," her crying mother had said to her all those years ago when she gave Autumn her father's wedding ring. "Take this."

"I don't want it!"

"Please. I know you're upset with Papa, but this will mean something to you one day." Mama had set the ring in her daughter's hand.

"No!" Twelve-year-old Autumn had thrown the ring to the floor. "I despise Papa! He left us!"

Autumn looked at the red postbox as she wept. Papa had left them, and she wasn't about to watch it happen again.

She took the two letters from her bag and dropped them in the box. Patience would be heartbroken. But this was for the best.

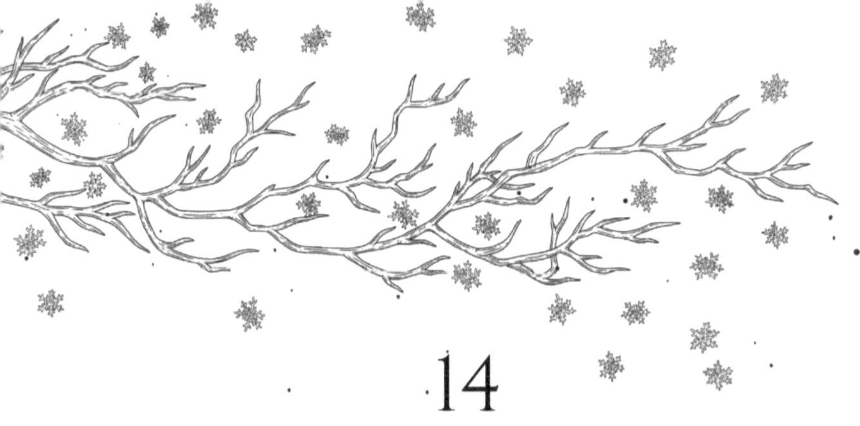

14

Autumn paced her bedroom the next day, nervously pulling on the edge of her long sleeve and biting at her lip. Sure enough, the letter had been delivered. Poor Patience had no idea what was coming.

On the bright side, life would be back to normal again soon, the way things were before the whole wretched affair began. After Patience opened the letter there would be tears, but Autumn would be there to dry them and they would make up with one another for good. They could start saving for a home of their own once more and, with time, the whole thing would be forgotten entirely.

Eventually Patience did arrive home; skipping down the dirt road, apparently singing a song while playing with the long strands of hair that had escaped the bun at the back of her head.

Autumn's stomach knotted. She couldn't possibly watch Patience open the envelope.

Perhaps she should run, run and take the envelope from her hand and shred it to pieces! No, it was too late for that.

Patience found the envelope on the kitchen table. She sighed with delight at the sight of the seal and squeezed the paper against her chest, closing her eyes. She tore open the letter before she'd removed her cloak. As she quickly read each line, her happy face slowly became confused. Her lower lip quivered, and she clapped a hand over her mouth.

Autumn, making a pretence of having just remembered something terribly important, ran upstairs to the bedroom to bury herself deep in her bedding and hide her face in shame. She was such an awful sister! She didn't deserve Patience. She should have stopped this, somehow, from ever happening.

Patience began to ascend the stairs, dragging her feet. Then she changed her mind, and trudged back down into the kitchen before she was even halfway up.

Autumn lifted her head from her blankets, listening. She couldn't stay here and cower any longer, not when her sister needed her now more than ever before. She washed her face and tidied herself before she descended the stairs, folding her arms tight to hide her shaking. She was terribly nervous.

A heartbroken Patience leaned against the doorway, her grip on the wooden doorframe slipping as she sank to the floor. The letter was back on the table.

"Patty?" Autumn's voice was a strained whisper.

Patience didn't move from the ground, only lifting her eyes upwards. They were dark and full of tears.

Autumn began to cry too, as she dropped to the floor and pulled her sister in close.

"Oh, oh Autumn. It's awful," Patience moaned, returning the embrace and pushing her face into her shoulder, soaking Autumn's collar with a cold hard weeping.

Autumn did her best to conceal her own grief. "What is it?"

"Mr. Williams..." Patience exploded into coughing.

Autumn waited and then asked as truthfully as she could, despite knowing well the answer to her question, "What has he done now?"

Patience covered her mouth with the back of one hand, body shivering as she clutched her sister tighter.

"It's okay! It's okay!" Autumn hugged her to soothe the trembling. "You will be all right now; don't you worry."

Patience gave her head a light shake, knitting her eyebrows together as she explained what Mr. Williams had written to her.

When Patience finished, Autumn cried even harder, not because Mr. Williams wouldn't be marrying Patience, but because she had deceived her poor sister. She had broken her sister's heart by writing her desired reality into existence, and there was nothing that she could do about it now.

Autumn stood and offered a hand to Patience, who accepted, rising without a sense of balance and falling back to her knees again. Crouching, she crossed her arms and hid her face.

"There, there," Autumn whispered, leaning down and rubbing her back. She sat on the floor beside Patience, realizing this would be a long day.

"I don't understand," Patience said after a while. "I thought he had changed. Especially after last night. I must have done something awful to provoke him, though I'm not sure what."

"There, there, Patty, don't trouble yourself. This won't have been your doing, but rather his own." They clung to one another again, and Autumn said with courage, "As much as it pains me to admit the truth, we are greatly blessed at the timing of his decision, which spares you severe public pain and humiliation. We must rejoice in the kindness of our fate, for the consequences may have been more severe had you already become Mrs. Williams."

"You are right," Patience whispered, pushing her head into her sister's chest, "and you always have been."

Autumn nodded, agreeing. However, even now, knowing that her happily ever after was secured, something deep inside twisted painfully. She pushed back the guilt, but it was no use. Patience was in a state of grief like nothing she had experienced before, and it was all Autumn's fault.

She had worked so hard to get to this moment; why did she feel so unhappy?

"There," Autumn put a checkered cloth over her finished sponge cake later that afternoon. That ought to cheer her sister up a little. The poor girl had gone off to her room some hours earlier to grieve and had yet to return.

Not having much else to do now that the baking was done, Autumn decided to do a bit of cleaning, starting with the windows. She took a wooden bucket, added water and vinegar, and proceeded to the sitting room. My, the windows were rather grimy!

Autumn separated the layers of some old newspapers, then took one sheet and dipped it in her solution.

She hauled the bucket up onto the kitchen table. The letter lay there still. She ran her finger in circles around the wax. *What have I done?* Autumn opened the door and looked out at the snow, which was no longer a perfect blanket but muddied with footprints.

"Miss Everleigh!"

Autumn rubbed away her tears, smiling in spite of herself at the approaching figure of Mr. Foster. She slipped on her cloak and went outside to greet him, not wishing to disturb Patience.

"Miss Everleigh!" he called again, frantically waving something in the air as he approached.

Autumn, delighted at the distraction from her woes, called out, laughing, "I am here!"

"My article!" he hollered, holding a paper above his head. "It's published!"

"It is?"

The air stung her face, and her heart raced, but she didn't care. "I want to see!" She snatched the paper away from his hold, needing proof he spoke the truth. "Oh! Those are your words right there!"

"Are they? I was afraid they were toying with me!"

Autumn smacked the paper as if to confirm. "Kendrick A. Foster!"

"A miracle, I must say!"

Autumn smiled and took up his hand. It was warm with excitement.

"Why I may even make it above the fold in the *Daily Telegraph*! Imagine the headline: *First Blind Man to Publish!* The shareholders shan't laugh at me anymore!"

"Who?"

"The men at the bank. I am headed there now to show them my success!"

"Must you leave so soon?" She cocked her head, pursing her lips.

"You are very welcome to accompany me, if you'd like."

Autumn did like; although she wanted to keep an eye on Patience, she was very glad of the opportunity to forget their worries for a moment. So, she agreed.

"You must put on something warmer!" she cautioned. "You shall freeze!"

"I haven't the time!" Mr. Foster stuffed the paper into his satchel.

And they went on in a hurry to the hectic streets of Carlisle, which were busier than ever with the holiday season in full swing.

Mr. Foster led the way, with Autumn struggling to keep up and having to stop every now and then to catch her breath and fix her hair, which kept coming undone. She was rather relieved when they finally reached the bank, a tall, regal building with thick pillars dominating a street corner. Customers walked in and out through the doors, above which 'S. F. Vault' was spelled out.

It was cold, probably too cold to snow. Autumn rubbed her hands together while Mr. Foster stomped the slush off his boots before entering the bank.

"Don't lose me now!" Autumn took hold of Mr. Foster's sleeve as he headed toward a set of stairs to the sidelines.

"Up we go."

Autumn followed, raising her voice to be heard among the crowd. "Do you work here often?"

"No. Not when I can help it. I do everything I can to stay away from the imbeciles who run this wretched place."

"If they are imbeciles, then why come here today?"

"They have been unspeakably cruel to me ever since I arrived here."

Autumn sighed, trying to keep up as Mr. Foster marched upward, far ahead of her with his satchel thumping against his side.

The booming excitement bellow faded when they reached the second-floor hallway, vacant save for a servant pushing a cart of meats and cheeses.

"Over here." Mr. Foster led Autumn to a set of double doors, tall and finely carved.

"Perhaps I should wait here until you finish. I doubt they shall be pleased with the presence of a woman in the workplace."

"Yes, but you are accompanying me. No one will comment."

Autumn assumed that special allowances were made due to his condition and aquiesced.

"Come now!" Mr. Foster shoved open the doors and burst in with such force that his foot caught on the edge of the carpet, and he lurched forward.

"Careful!" Autumn warned, but it was too late. Mr. Foster fell to his shins, then got back up in a hurry and dusted off his knees.

The room proved to be quite large, full of bookshelves surrounding a gathering of five or so old men sitting in big chairs around a low table laden with tea and cakes.

"Gentlemen!" said Mr. Foster, standing tall and resetting his figure.

"You had better get that energy out of your step or you will blow us all away," said one of the men in a slow, steady voice as he took his eyes from the notebook in hand to scowl at the newcomers.

"Don't be dull, Mr. Brawley." Mr. Foster smiled. "Take a chair of your choosing, Miss Everleigh."

"Who is this?" asked Mr. Brawley. The seated men fixed their eyes on Autumn, who gave a tight smile and seated herself in a wooden chair at the back of the room near a desk with a green lamp. She folded her hands in her lap, not wanting to be judged.

"This is Miss Everleigh, and she is not to be minded."

Everyone appeared content with this answer, save for one man who frowned and put out his cigar.

"As I was saying, before we were interrupted," Mr. Brawley said pointedly, turning his attention back to the group. "Our consumer debt has skyrocketed this holiday season as more and more customers request extensions on their loans!"

"Indeed," another frayed voice said solemnly. "I overheard a man at the barbershop saying he won't be able to make a payment before the new year under his current circumstances."

"Exactly," Mr. Brawley said, in a quieter voice. "Mr. Foster, won't you please sit down?"

Mr. Foster stood leaning over the table, bag clasped in his hands. "Yes. Of course." And he sank into an empty seat, scratching his chin and giving little nods.

"With that being said, I have devised a plan," continued Mr. Brawley, and Autumn flinched as he slammed a fist on the table, causing the teacups to rattle against their saucers.

"It's a good plan, too," another man said, speaking up for the first time. His tone was somewhat malicious. He didn't look quite as fragile as the others and appeared to be several decades younger than the rest.

Mr. Brawley went on, "If the citizens can't make their payments by the end of the month, we dismiss them and make way for paying customers. The housing market is in high demand, with new families coming to Brampton, Wigtown and Carlisle all the time. The problem? All the houses are currently occupied. So, if we eject the current owners, who cannot pay, while also raising the interest by, I don't know, say a mere ten percent, we will draw in the wealthier crowd who can meet the pay. The best part? We see profits *now*."

Everyone murmured among themselves, whispering and making stray comments to each other.

"Let's vote."

One of the chairs creaked.

Autumn focused on the pulsing flames of the fireplace behind Mr. Brawley, wishing she could leave.

Mr. Brawley cleared his throat. "All in favour of the proposed plan to raise the interest rates and foreclose the properties, say aye."

"Aye!" the men shouted in unison, save for Mr. Foster, who went on tapping his chin and saying nothing at all.

Autumn wondered what was wrong with him. The room grew silent, and Mr. Foster turned his head both ways.

"Well?" he asked, "aren't we going to finish our discussion? Didn't you have something of importance you were talking about before I came in?"

Mr. Brawley's voice deepened, pure annoyance driving his speech. "I don't know where you have been, but we have already devised our course of action and the popular vote has won."

"What about my say?" Mr. Foster crossed one leg over the other and crossed his arms.

"Doesn't much matter, you would have been one to five had you voted against us. Now tell me, where has your head been this blasted afternoon? First, you trot in giddy as a goat, bringing unwanted company, and now you seem to be paying very little attention. Have you been at the Christmas sherry already?"

"No sir, I have not had a cup of cheer, but something rather better! Gentlemen!" He stood from his seat and set his shoulders. "I have some exciting news to share with you all! So long as you don't mind, that is..."

"Go on; you have already disrupted us twice. You might as well continue."

"Well, then!" Mr. Foster grinned, pointing a finger at the roof. "As none of you know, I have been working very hard behind the scenes these last months, writing an article." As he spoke, he walked around the circle of men, every step strong and purposeful. "I spent many long hours using my talents to write and describe everything good about life to put it to paper in the form of a short story, if you will." He paused. The men said nothing. Mr. Foster went on, rummaging around in his bag, producing the newspaper. "After all my weeks of hard work, I have done it!" He fumbled around and gripped the table with his free hand, setting a triumphant foot atop the surface with a *thud!*

Everyone gasped, including Autumn. "Mr. Foster," she whispered, eyebrows raised. "What are you doing?"

"Here it is, my friends! My article! I am now a published author and am just as capable as any of you! You haven't a need to mock me anymore. No, sir. I am equal!" And with that Mr. Foster made his way back to his chair, breathing heavily, and sat with an air of authority and an open-mouthed smile. "Well?" He turned his head from side to side while crossing his arms as if waiting for applause of approval or even a few handshakes; none came.

Mr. Brawley lifted a stack of uneven papers and tapped them on the table a few times, then set them back into place. "How does this benefit the company, exactly?" He spoke as if his words were obvious and Mr. Foster a poorly behaved child.

"Oh, it doesn't," he began, lightly. "You see, it's my—"

"If it bears no importance to the company, I should say it doesn't really matter, and if it doesn't matter, then we can move on to other, more important topics. Gentleman! Let us continue with—"

Mr. Foster was undeterred, "No, you don't understand." He shook his head, lifted his newspaper and slapped his fingers against the front. "I didn't write this just so you could all act as if I hadn't."

"If I had wanted two minutes of my life wasted, I would have asked for someone more entertaining. Now, on the subject of loans—"

"No!"

"I beg your pardon?"

"I said no!"

"Mr. Foster. I have kindly tried to move on from the matter once, twice, and this will be my final request."

"You fail to comprehend I wrote this article myself! My writing was accepted and published by the *Daily Post*, yet all you have to say is absolutely nothing?" He waved his cherished newspaper again, and Mr. Brawley snatched it from his hands.

"*No!*" Autumn shrieked, rising to her feet as the cruel man crumpled the paper into a ball and tossed it into the laughing fireplace.

Mr. Foster didn't say anything. He turned his ear in the direction of the flames, as if still grasping what had happened.

"Imbeciles!" He slammed his fists on the table and rose, knocking over his chair. "All of you!" He went to the exit, fiddling the knob with aggression and sending the door crashing against the wall. "Complete and utter imbeciles!"

"Mr. Foster!" Autumn collected her skirts and hurried after him.

Mr. Foster was already heading down the flight of stairs, missing most steps on the way and tripping more than twice.

"Mr. Foster!" Autumn followed him to the ground floor, pushing through a stuffy collection of clients to keep up. "Wait!" She threw out her hand as he disappeared in the crowd. "Excuse me!" Autumn pushed between two men. "Sorry—" she squeezed her way to the entrance, leaving the building and grateful for some fresh air.

"What did I do wrong?" Mr. Foster asked. He continued to hurry down the pavement. The first flakes of a fresh snowfall clung to his shoulders.

"Mr. Foster!"

"I worked so hard, and nothing! No return on investment whatsoever! They couldn't see past me then, and they still can't now!"

"Mr. Foster!"

He stopped walking and turned around. "No, Miss Everleigh! They are fools for ignoring the emotion behind my self-worth!"

"You are right. And what they did was just dastardly, though I plead that you take but a moment and listen to yourself."

"I am always listening! All I ever do is listen! There must be someone who cares for all I have accomplished..."

"Oh, ho ho!" jeered a fat little boy from the street, pulling a sled by the ropes. "Has one of the three blind mice wandered away from his pack?"

"Child!" Mr. Foster faced the direction the boy's voice had come from. "You'll never guess what I have done! I have an article featured in the newspaper, which makes my contribution in life so much more than you or *anyone* could have ever imagined." And Mr. Foster laughed to himself, bending over and slapping his knees.

The boy packed a snowball together and sent it flying into Mr. Foster's back with perfect aim.

"Blind *and* crazy! Well, you aren't going to find any cheese here, little mouse!" And the boy disappeared down the street to join his friends who were running and laughing at his cruel jest.

"Come back here," Mr. Foster shook a fist, fury in his tone. "And bring your friends! Tell them all I have achieved and spread the good news!"

Autumn shook her head, eyebrows knitted as she stooped and rolled a snowball, sending it colliding with Mr. Foster's face. "That is quite enough!"

"Ugh!" He spat, wiping his eyes but not managing to clean away the moisture.

Autumn stepped forward and wrapped her fingers over both his arms, gazing up into his face with soft, caring eyes.

"I..." he whispered, at last beginning to calm himself. "I thought I could earn their affection. I don't know what I did wrong..."

Autumn cried for him, her voice cracking. "Maybe you shouldn't be chasing the love of the people who were never going to love you anyway."

He squeezed his lids shut, hesitating as if considering her words. "No. That's crazy. I have agonised long enough. I deserve praise."

Autumn pulled down on his arm and stood on tiptoes, placing her gentle lips on his cold cheek, holding them there for a moment.

"The world doesn't have to adore you, Kendrick. Sometimes all you need is one person."

He said nothing as his throat quivered.

She drew away, putting her hands over his. "I'll leave you now." And she left, not looking back.

15

It had been only a day since Patience had opened the letter. At first, the girl seldom spoke and sat staring blankly or quietly sobbing. Later, Patience wished to go to Mr. Williams and beg him to reconsider, but Autumn had forbidden the meeting, telling her that his words strictly said his mind couldn't be changed.

The morning started off promising. The sisters woke early and bundled themselves up in their warmest winter attire to go down to the lake and watch the sunrise in their favourite spot. It had been weeks since they'd last visited and the fresh air seemed to do Patience good. Afterward, they came home, and Autumn went out to tackle the dishes. The plates stretched to the ceiling, threatening to topple over at any given moment and come shattering to the ground.

Autumn found a dishcloth and scrubbed away, popping the occasional bubble with a finger as the spheres floated through the air. She let her thoughts consume her. Poor Mr. Foster. He had been so hopeless. If only he understood how truly worthy he was of love.

There was a knock at the front door. Autumn stopped scrubbing and looked out the window to see a grand, two-horse carriage glistening in the afternoon sun as it came to a halt.

"Goodness!" She wiped her soapy fingers on a dishcloth and ran to fix her hair, hoping that her surprise guest was Mr. Foster in a better temper at that perhaps he wished to speak with her about... well.

Despite Autumn trying to pull herself together, she forgot to take off her apron and looked rather like a housemaid in the middle of her daily chores.

She finished fastening her hair and opened the door to find two middle-aged men standing on her front porch. They each had a mustache, an expensive suit, and a strong scent of expensive cologne rolling off their shoulders.

"Gentlemen," she said, taking a deep, troubled breath. She was too surprised to be disappointed.

"Hello," the man with spectacles said. "Is Mr. Everleigh here?"

"Oh, no... there is no Mr. Everleigh. Only me, and my younger sister."

"Then you must be Miss Everleigh, I presume?" He put a finger on his clipboard. "Autumn, is it?"

"Why—yes, that's right. Whatever is the matter?" She pulled at the tip of her pointer finger and eyed the two men.

"Miss," said the other, unable to keep eye contact. "We are here on behalf of the bank to notify you of the recent price increases on your property."

"Whatever do you mean?"

"That the bank is increasing your monthly payments by ten percent."

"Ten percent! But sir, we can hardly afford to pay as it is let alone give any extra."

"Then in that case we must deliver this." He handed her an eviction notice.

"No!" Autumn's face crumpled as the men bowed their heads and left.

Her eyes took in the writing as she cried. She couldn't lose her home! Not again. Her remaining savings would never survive under such prices. No. She would lose her home unless she found some other way. The only person she knew to ask was Mrs. Glendale. She must go to her and explain everything. She would ask for extra payment and commit to working overtime by giving Hazel extra dance lessons. It was her only hope.

Autumn fetched her thick cloak, draping it over her shoulders before braving the dreadful winter cold. A nasty wind circulated the air that day, its fingers creeping inside her cloak and tangling her hair in knots.

"You are all right… you are all right…" she whispered to herself in a song while trudging through the copse. She would be okay; Mrs. Glendale would understand.

When she arrived at the Raven's Nest, her fingers were numb and shaking, and her face felt raw with cold. Snow lay everywhere, dusted over the grass and trees and sleeping on the roof. Fluffy smoke expanded from each of the many chimneys.

Autumn stumbled to the back door and let herself in. Warmth enveloped her frigid body as she stepped into the dimly lit servants' quarters, where maids bustled around carrying dirty clothes and cleaning supplies. Autumn moved to the hall, stepping to the side as two men carrying a large pine tree passed.

"This way, easy does it." Mr. Williams commanded, waving his arms to direct the tree into the dining room. He did not notice Autumn. His eyes were red and he looked extremely tired.

Autumn retreated quickly, glad he had not spotted her. It would be best to avoid him, for the time being at least. After all, she might accidentally reveal something she wished to remain confidential.

Many strips of garland clothed the white staircase in the entryway, decorated with popcorn and speckles of holly. Autumn bent down and lifted a fallen pine sprig from the floor and inhaled the rich scent. Delicious! She must cut down a tree with Patience tomorrow and collect their Christmas decorations from the cellar.

A door shut above Autumn's head, and she shifted her attention to the staircase to see Mr. Foster hurrying down, wearing his suit as always, although this time with a dark red cravat around his neck. His hair was not as neat as usual.

"Mr. Foster," Autumn said, for once not in a hurry to be with him.

"Miss Everleigh!" He smiled, appearing happier than yesterday as he ran his fingers along his chin. "How fortunate this is. I was just on my way to speak with you!"

She fingered the pine needles in her hand and glanced down the hall. "I am afraid I myself am in a hurry to discuss something with Mrs.

Glendale. I shall seek you out once I've met with her." And she headed away.

"Yes, well, I wanted to apologise for the way I acted at the bank yesterday and—"

"Mr. Foster, I shall be yours to enjoy in but a moment's time. If you would only excuse me for now."

He spoke no further, but merely nodded. Autumn ventured into the parlour, a generous room displaying a single pillar and marble floors without carpet. Handsome ivory curtains hung around a set of couches and a single bench.

"Mrs. Glendale?" Autumn gasped when she stepped in, finding the older woman seated in the middle of the yellow couch with her face hidden in her dress. She was crying. "My goodness, are you well?" Autumn hastened over, seating herself beside the lady and placing a hand over her unsteady back. Mr. Foster entered and moved near the fireplace.

Mrs. Glendale raised a weak head. Her skin was blotchy, her eyelids sagged and faint wrinkles near her lower nose and lips had appeared.

"I know you did it," she whispered.

Autumn choked on her words.

"D-did what?"

Mrs. Glendale lifted a paper from beside her, showing Autumn the letter she had penned and posted to Mr. Williams.

"It must have been you."

Autumn blinked hard, speaking with haste, "Mrs. Glendale, with all due respect, I have no idea what you are speaking of."

"I asked so nicely." Mrs. Glendale used a soft tone full of sadness as she set a hand over Autumn's hand. "I asked you to leave them alone, and yet you proceeded to take my Percy away from me."

"Percy?" Autumn spoke gently and steadily, despite her fear. "I have never met anyone named Percy."

"He was our brother. I killed him."

Autumn's heart stopped as the overwrought older woman gulped frantic breaths, putting a hand to her neck. She rocked forwards, overcome.

"Shhh," Autumn soothed. "It's all right."

Mrs. Glendale made choking noises as if food were clogged in her throat, tears dripping over her fingers. "I have suffered many years knowing I drowned him. It was an accident. It *was* an accident. We were playing, one of our silly adventure games, in the pond at Perlyn Hall. I have suffered through marriage... and having children of my own. You think I desired the curse of children? No... Lord, no. The last thing I ever wanted was to be near another child, lest I hurt them as I hurt poor, poor Percy!"

Autumn wanted to comfort Mrs. Glendale, but knew not what to say. The woman looked at her as she went on,

"Can you imagine the incomparable pain of looking into the eyes of your own daughter and seeing the one you lost? The pain of knowing you don't deserve them? The pain of suffering as I watch Clarence visit the very countries we pretended to explore together as children, always being reminded of those happy days..."

Autumn herself felt she might cry all of a sudden. She spoke gently to the distraught Mrs. Glendale, "I am not sure I understand. Why do you tell me all this now?"

"My dear, dear brother died at Perlyn Hall, and once my parents passed, Clarence inherited the estate for himself. He knows how much I want it. He knows how much I miss, miss, miss, *miss* him. And being the good man his is, he promised to give me Perlyn after he found a wife. I was so close. Percy was going to be okay, and then you... you wrote this letter to separate them! Do you have not a care in the world for what you've done to me?"

"I- I had no idea," Autumn whispered, face crumpling as she gave way to tears.

"I did. And I am afraid I have let Percy down again. I should have stopped you when I had the chance."

"Please," Autumn's voice box throbbed. "Don't tell them what I have done. I can make all this right if you only give me the chance to do so. Please." Autumn closed her eyes and clutched Mrs. Glendale's hand, desperately pleading.

When Autumn looked up at Mrs. Glendale, her eyes had shifted behind Autumn, to the door. "I shan't have to tell them. I think she already knows."

"Autumn?" said Patience, voice hoarse.

Autumn pressed her lips together and rose on unsteady feet to face her sister.

Patience stood in the doorway; her face was extremely pale and bloodless but her eyes were aflame.

"Patty, it—it's not like that," Autumn reached her hand out toward her sister. "I didn't write the letters to harm you, honestly."

Patience advanced closer, her eyes burning coals. She did not speak.

"I am so sorry."

Patience tore the paper from Mrs. Glendale to wave in her sibling's face. "You ruined me! You ripped me from my love! I wouldn't do a thing like that to my most hated enemy. How could you?"

Autumn squeezed her teeth together, biting down to ease the pain of her heart. "I was scared! I was scared you weren't ready and I was scared I would lose you! Your protection was the uppermost—"

"Protection? Protecting yourself! And just when I thought that you were right about everything..." Her head shook in jerky movements in her anger. Autumn had never seen her so furious.

"Patience, I—"

Patience raised her gaze and silenced her sister. "You have lost me, Autumn. There is nothing now you can do that will ever change that."

Autumn watched her sister storm from the room. She sat down on the couch once again, her eyes fixed on the place where Patience had stood.

"Miss Everleigh." Mr. Foster took a step toward her. "This is all my fault."

Autumn turned to Mrs. Glendale, too shocked to cry.

"You saw the stamp... is that how you knew?"

Mrs. Glendale hid her face again, voice muffled. "Yes. Mr. Foster told me to give it to you; I put it in the box myself."

"Mr. Foster—" Autumn stood, the enormity of her grief weighing heavy on her shoulders. Mr. Foster was a traitor. How could he do this to her? She sniffed again.

"Miss Everleigh—"

"How could you?" Autumn snarled through her teeth, forgetting Mrs. Glendale entirely. "You promised not to tell anyone!"

"I swear I forgot."

"You are always forgetting!" Her voice rose. "I trusted you!"

"Miss Everleigh—" He stepped towards her, searching for her hand.

"This is all your fault!" She pushed him with full force, sending him tripping backward.

"It was an honest mistake, I would never—"

But Autumn could not bear to hear his explanation, "That makes nothing right. I have lost everything! My house is gone, Patience will never speak to me again, and it's all your fault!" She stomped into the hall and he followed close behind, still reaching for her.

"You are right; it *is* my fault. I swear I will do everything within my power to restore all you've lost. I will speak with your sister and with Mrs. Glendale and, and use my position to persuade them to be at peace with you. And once your connections are restored, I will pay for your home. I will give you enough fortune to live contently in it as long as you wish."

He took Autumn by the arm and together the two moved across the hall and entered a sitting room. It was dark save for a single oil lamp lighting the space. Autumn pulled away from his touch as soon as they were alone.

"Do you only make promises you don't intend to keep?"

"Not at all."

"How on earth could you ever keep this one? Are you planning on robbing the bank? Perhaps you—"

Mr. Foster spoke in a great rush now, "The Ivory. It's mine. I am the master of the home. I own the S. F. Vault, my late uncle's bank, the Simon Foster Vault. I am not a poor man but rather a wealthy one hiding a handsome collection of riches. I have deceived those around me, I have deceived you, Miss Everleigh, to have a chance of being... of being seen as something more than I truly am."

Autumn froze. She stared at him, unable to move due to shock. He had tricked her. He was not the man she thought he was. He was the man she had anticipated from the very beginning: a liar, a breaker of promises, and a deceiver. He really was just like everyone else. Just like her father.

"I don't want to believe you." She stared into his eyes, wishing she had heard him incorrectly, wishing he would laugh and say it was a joke. "With... with the feelings I have, I really do not want to believe that you would lie to me, Mr. Foster."

"Miss Everleigh, I have only ever told you one lie in our acquaintance. I lied when I said I worked for Mr. Lawrence, and that was a mistake. I lied because I was afraid you would see me differently if you knew my position. I see that was foolish of me now."

"You said you gave your wealth away to Clarinda!"

"I did. Just... not quite all of it."

Autumn was too hurt to hide her pain. "I let down my guard for you, did you know that? For the first time in my life, for the first time since I was a child. I cannot tell you how hard that was. I thought you were different. I foolishly trusted you, as I have never trusted anyone else, and that was a terrible, terrible mistake."

"You must know the reason I lied was because I... well, I was extremely fond of you. And now, now I love you. In every sense of the word. I have tossed and turned ever since we went to Perlyn, thinking of how to tell you how I feel."

Autumn stood as still as a statue. She breathed and she blinked but otherwise moved not a muscle.

"I should have come to you with my feelings sooner, but I feared losing you as I did Clarinda. I have been blind... not in sight, but in mind. You were quite right: I do not need the world to love me, or even to accept me, Miss Everleigh. But I do need you. And if you will only allow me to fix what I have broken, I promise I will never again deceive you for as long as either of us shall live. You say you allowed yourself to trust me and I must confess I trusted you the very moment I heard your voice. More than anything. If you will only do me the honour of granting me a chance to prove myself, I will ensure you are happy and safe for all the days of your life."

Autumn finally moved. She drew near to him, closing her eyes. She moved so close to Mr. Foster that she could feel his breath upon her cheek. He smelled faintly of peanut brittle.

"I... I cannot." She pulled away so quickly she upset the table and something crashed to the ground. They paid no attention. "Not after what you have done. You have lied once; therefore, you could lie again. Prove me wrong!"

Mr. Foster's eyes went dark. "So, it's true..."

"What is? That I shall live in misery for the rest of my days? You think I want to be angry with you?"

A fire crackled beside her. The oil lamp lay on the carpet, broken. Flame from the wick was spreading across the rug.

"Oh, no," her voice cracked. "What have I done?" Autumn focused on the fire, her anger forgotten. The fire was spreading so quickly she had to hop out of the way to avoid being burned.

"Mr. Foster, come quick!" She took his hand as he muttered little phrases under his breath, as if in a trance.

"Quickly, please!" She tugged on him as she passed through the doorway, hand slipping from his. "Fire!" She called into the hall. "Fire! Someone get help! Mr. Foster…"

"I knew it," he whispered under his breath, head bowed.

"Whatever are you talking about? Come, we must go now!"

The fire crept over the rug behind him, the heat rising. Still, he stood. His face was wet with tears. "I knew I was not worthy of love."

A sharp pain pierced Autumn's heart as her mind contradicted his words. What was she thinking? Of course, she loved him. She was just upset, not so much with him as with herself. Mr. Foster was more than worthy of love. She loved him as she had loved no other person on earth other than her dear sister. He had made some mistakes but so had she.

"Don't be a fool!" she said, taking his hand. "You must know that I—"

"Goodbye, Autumn." He gave her hand a last squeeze and stepped back, pushing her away from him.

She lost her balance and fell backward to land on the hall floor.

"Oh!" When she looked up, the door was already closed. She heard the key turn in the lock.

"No!" She scrambled to her feet and flung herself against the door, twisting the handle until she tore the skin from the palms of her hand.

"Mr. Foster!" The door stayed firmly shut. "Don't do this!"

A teary Mrs. Glendale entered the hall from the parlour. "What is happening now?"

Autumn collapsed to the floor in a huddle, barely able speak. "F-f-fire!"

"Lord have mercy. Clarence!" Mrs. Glendale shrieked. "Clarence, come quickly!"

An uproar of commotion sounded throughout the downstairs as servants arrived, shoving past the emotional women. A baffled Mr. Williams appeared, eyebrows knitted and pine needles scattered across his clothes.

"Mr. Williams!" Autumn coughed, waving her hand to flag him down.

He hastened over and lifted her to her feet as she threw all her weight into him. "Mr. Williams!" She sobbed as he helped stabilise her in a hug.

"Tell me, tell what has happened!"

"He's trapped!"

"Who's trapped?"

"Mr. Foster. In there, in there. Oh please, please..."

The fire crackled from within as two servants slammed their weight at the door, opening it with a splitting crack. Smoke spilled into the hall.

Mr. Williams sprang into action, guiding Autumn to his sister and throwing his coat to the side. "I will be right back." He kissed Mrs. Glendale's cheek, and she grasped his hand in her own.

"No, no, it's too dangerous! I can't lose—"

"I promise." He spoke sternly but smiled as he slipped his hand away, then set his shoulders and plunged into the burning room.

"Oh!" Mrs. Glendale sank her head against Autumns chest. They held each other up, Mrs. Glendale weeping and Autumn so shocked she could barely breathe.

Servants and maids followed Mr. Williams in one after the other, creating a chain of buckets and pouring cold water over the fire. "Keep it coming!" Mr. Williams called.

Autumn's eyes stung from the smoke. *Please, please be all right. Please be safe. Oh, please.*

"We need more water!"

"Move!"

"Out of my way!" Mr. Williams backed out of the door, his clothes and face dark with soot. "Clear the way!" He turned, staggering past servants, carrying the limp body of Mr. Foster in his arms as the smoke cleared.

"Oh!" Autumn stumbled forward, gripping Mr. Williams' shoulder and following as her love was laid to the floor.

"Mr. Foster...?" she dropped to his side, hands hovering over his still form. "I am so sorry," she whispered, lowering her forehead against his. "So, so sorry."

Autumn didn't move for some time, hardly noticing what was going on around her. She only trembled and wetted Mr. Foster's face with her tears. This was all her fault.

"Miss Everleigh?" Mr. Williams put a hand on her shoulder, using a soothing voice. "The fire is out. He is going to be all right; a doctor is on the way."

Autumn nodded, squeezing her lips together in hopes of soothing the pain as she stood, keeping her gaze on Mr. Foster's precious face. This was all too much. Besides, she was no longer needed; Mr. Foster was breathing, and the servants were all busy fanning away the last of the smoke and carrying away the burned rug as Mr. Williams comforted his sister. *Look at what I've done... it is I who is unworthy of love!* Autumn tore away in tears, fleeing for the back door.

16

Autumn picked up her pace as she ran out of the Raven's Nest and into the copse.

All was lost. Her home, Mrs. Glendale's respect and probably her job, Mr. Foster, and most importantly, Patience, her only reason for existence.

Autumn's cloak came unclipped as she ran and flew away in the breeze before falling in the snow. She didn't even bother to go back for it. It didn't matter if she froze.

As she fled through the trees her own words rang through her head. *Patience, stop running! If you fall, you'll skin your knees!*

She shook her old reprimand out of her mind only to have another fill the void. *Patience, how many times must I tell you to be more careful?*

You could injure yourself! Another particular day popped into her mind. Patience was only eight years old and spinning in circles in a field.

"Patience!" fourteen-year-old Autumn had said to her.

"Yes, Autty?"

"Don't spin so, you could trip and hurt yourself!"

Young Patience's face had fallen, sadness filling her gaze.

Autumn moaned at the memory as she moved in and out of the trees; she was ashamed of herself. She had hurt her sister for so long. How had she never realised?

Autumn's hair came undone and flapped behind her, catching in stray branches and foliage. Her cheeks stung from the cold. It felt like needles against her skin.

She quickened her pace, passing a tree as her foot caught on the ground and sent her flying forward.

"Oh!" Her face plummeted into the deep snow. Cold ate at her eyes. She lifted her head, rolled over and sat up, groaning. She wiped the snow from her face, fingers growing stiff. She smacked her tongue and let her hands drag at the wrists as she stood to her feet. As soon as she stood, pain shot up her left leg, causing her to fall again.

"Ah!" Autumn yelped. She tried to stand again, putting less pressure on her left foot this time. She winced, then fell back into the snow once again. She leaned forward and felt her ankle, which was very painful to her touch.

Autumn tried to stand again, this time only on her heel. The pain protested again, sending her sprawling into the snow. She couldn't walk; she could hardly move.

Autumn moaned over and over as she lay there, helplessly. She cupped her hands around her injured ankle.

The wind howled through the trees, sending goose bumps down her arms. She would freeze if she stayed out here much longer. *I should have gone back for that wretched cloak.*

"Help!" she called into the copse. "Someone! Anyone! I am hurt!" She stopped to listen.

Nothing. Snow began to sift from the sky like powdered sugar dusting her nose.

"*Help!*" She called again, trying to stand. She couldn't, and fell into the snow. She sat, hugging her knees.

This was probably what she deserved for all she had done to her sister. She had been so overprotective all those years and then she had separated her from Mr. Williams. Autumn would now die out here alone. Die just like her father had, after losing a home and leaving behind his family. And to think, after Autumn had spent her entire life trying to prevent someone from harming her. In the end, she had been the one to betray herself. She had trusted herself with the task of keeping her and Patience safe, and this is where she had ended up.

Autumn set her forehead on her knees and closed her eyes, allowing the frost to consume her body. She sniffed. No one would miss her now, not even her own sister.

A soft rustle on the tips of the breeze tapped the air and danced like snowflakes in her ears. At first, Autumn thought it was the trees swaying to and fro, but as she listened, she realised it was a human voice, singing. She raised her head and strained her ears, keeping as still as possible. The singing grew louder with each verse, though still distant.

"Hum ditty, hum ditty, off in a daydream,

Won't you come and dance with me?

Hum ditty, hum ditty, off in a daydream,

Won't you come and dance with me?"

Autumn cried at hearing her sister's unmistakable voice and lifted her own to join in:

"Hey oh, the whirlwind blows

Through the highs and through the lows.

Hey oh, the whirlwind blows

And sweeps us 'til the sun comes down."

They sang together, Autumn clutching her heart and blinking through her clouded sight as Patience walked through the trees, drawing near as they finished their song.

"Hum ditty, hum ditty, off in a daydream,

Won't you come and dance with me?

Hum ditty, hum ditty, off in a daydream,

Thank you for the dance with me..."

Patience approached her sister with a thick winter cloak over her shoulders and blonde hair sprinkled with white flakes, nose pink and eyes teary.

"Patience," Autumn choked, "I am so, so—"

"Shh, now," Patience bent down, voice airy. "What's happened?"

"I think I've sprained my ankle. I can't move."

Patience started to lift her sister.

"No, I don't need your help." She tightened her muscles as her teeth chattered.

"Yes," Patience whispered, with a sad laugh, "you do."

A tear slipped down Autumn's cheek, and she nodded while gesturing to her injury.

Patience went to work, cautiously pulling off Autumn's left boot and the soaked stocking and setting both aside. "Your ankle is swollen."

Autumn examined the damage and shuddered.

Patience lifted the cloak from her own shoulders and wrapped it around her sister. "Keep warm." She bent down and clutched a section of her own dress and ripped, tearing the fabric and pulling away most of the hem.

Autumn watched, mouth open, as Patience headed down to the trickling stream to dip the cloth in. She soon returned and lowered herself into the damp snow beside Autumn.

"Here." Patience lifted her leg into her lap and started dabbing the cloth over the injury with slow movements.

Autumn blinked in wonder, as her sister whispered words of care in her ear and went about wrapping the wound.

"There, there, you are quite brave, you know?" Patience said. "You will feel much better soon."

Autumn sniffed miserably.

Patience had grown up. She was no longer the child Autumn thought her to be.

Patience slid the damp stocking onto her foot and gently put the boot back on. "You are going to be just fine." She smiled with tired eyes as she hugged her sister. "I am just so sorry for all I have done."

"You are not the one who should apologise," Autumn shook her head, "for I have been quite the worst sister. Perhaps the worst in the world."

"You've been very stubborn, as have I." Patience ran a hand over Autumn's trembling back. The two sat there, shivering and holding onto one another to keep the other warm.

Autumn's head grew weary, and she rested it atop her sister's shoulder. "You do not understand... for I was so afraid of anyone hurting us that I lost what meant most to me. Not some house or ridiculous thing, but you. You, Patience! You are all that really matters. And I used to think you were so naïve. But look at you," she said, pointing to her leg. "You have grown up."

Patience, who's eyes were growing wetter by the minute, burst into sobs. "Autumn, you must not take all the blame. For I have been just as thoughtless. Oh, Autty." She moaned, covering her mouth with her open palm. "Autumn, I've been so terribly selfish. I chose to pursue my dreams over our family, knowing it would harm you. I didn't mean to do it, honestly! It just happened. Slowly, then all of a sudden. Before I knew it, it was too late! This is all my fault." She buried her face in her lap, crying harder.

"Dear Patty," Autumn reached for her sister's hand, "don't fret so. You had good reason. I realise now, I have never let you be your own person. I kept you from making your own decisions because I didn't think you were capable of making choices for yourself, and that was wrong. That was very wrong."

Patience crossed her legs and bent forward, using her hands to slowly get up. "Autumn," she reached down, taking Autumn's hands and helping her to stand, "you are not the worst sister in the world."

Autumn shrugged, using her sister for stability and letting her gaze fall to the ground.

Patience smiled as she went on. "You spent your entire life striving to keep me safe because you love me. You didn't focus on yourself but, instead, cared for your sister. It isn't just anyone who would do that."

"I suppose so."

"Although sometimes fear gets the better of us, twisting everything to seem like a threat. That is not what life is about, though."

"You got the worst of my actions, I am sure. I do not blame you for your behaviour."

"I was wrong, too. I just wish you would have told me how you felt, how you really felt, sooner."

Autumn nodded, lifting her gaze to meet her sister's loving eyes. "Patience?" She tilted her head a little to the left.

"Yes, Autumn?" Patience said, giving a few quick blinks.

"How is it I am lucky enough to have you in my life?"

"I ask myself that all the time about you."

They squeezed one another in a tight embrace, crying with joy.

"From now on," Autumn tightened her hold, "We shall meet in the middle."

"In the space between the seasons."

They left the hug, and held on to each other's hands, intertwining their fingers.

"I love you," Patience said, eyes twinkling.

"I love you, too."

They stood still, eyes saying more than words as Autumn's heart lifted.

"Autty, I want you to know that even if we straighten out our mishaps with the others, I will not marry Mr. Williams. Our relationship is too valuable to risk losing again."

Autumn smiled faintly and held back her tears. She knew what she had to do, though her soul shook inside. "Well," she heaved, giving her sister's hand a squeeze. "I'm going to miss you," her voice cracked.

"Why, you're not going anywhere, are you?" Patience asked, voice shaking.

"No." Autumn smiled as well as she was able, despite her emotions.

"I'm not going anywhere, am I?"

"Yes," Autumn nodded, biting down on her lower lip, hot tears spilling down her face, "You are. You are going to marry the wonderful, charming and deserving Mr. Williams. And I'm going to miss you for every one of the minutes I can't be with you."

"Autumn, no! I can't!"

"Mr. Williams loves you," she said, tapping Patience on the nose. "He would never let anything bad happen to you."

"I promise," Patience whispered. "I will always come back as often as I can." She hugged her sister tighter. "Although I beg you to come on our journeys with us. Promise you'll try?"

"So long as you never grow tired of me."

"Oh, how could we, Autty!" Patience giggled.

"Okay. I promise."

Autumn stroked her sister's hair, eyes following her fingers as they swept across the blonde strands. "Well. Shall we be going?"

"I certainly wouldn't mind some extra warmth about now," she laughed.

Autumn laughed too and hobbled painfully along as Patience supported all her weight.

Though they were slow, given Autumn's ankle, and rather cold in that moment, a peace filled Autumn's soul for the first time since she could remember.

The sisters went on through the copse, growing weaker with every step.

"We are so close," Patience whispered, smiling.

"Yes, we shall be near a roaring fire in no time..."

The end of the copse was within sight when a voice called out to them, "Miss Everleigh!"

Both sisters exchanged grateful glances. "Mr. Williams! Over here!"

"Where?"

"Here!"

He soon neared them, face lighting up. "Why did you run off?"

"She sprained her ankle!"

"My God," he said, putting a hand on Autumn's cheek. "You are freezing!" He wasted no time in scooping her up in his arms. "Come, we must get you both inside and dry."

The three huddled close together, and Autumn was impressed by his ability to carry her without a break. He didn't stop until they arrived at the Raven's Nest.

"You found them," Mrs. Glendale said when they arrived, relief evident on her face as she opened the door.

"Throw some logs on the fire," directed Mr. Williams to a servant, and soon Autumn and Patience were sitting on the floor in the drawing room next to the crackling flames, much warmer now and sharing a large blanket.

"You are sure that Mr. Foster is quite all right?" Autumn asked.

Mr. Williams nodded. "The doctor is with him now. The poor fellow has finally woken up."

Autumn nodded, quite thankful.

"I missed all the fun," Patience giggled, sneezing.

"Bless you," Autumn said. "Yes, I am afraid I was the cause of most of the excitement." She let her eyes fix on Mr. Williams, who only paced the room. She opened her mouth to speak.

"You don't have to say anything," he said, coming to a halt.

"Oh, but I want to! Mr. Williams, I have so much I wish to apologise for! For making assumptions about your personality, for sending the letters, for forging your seal and, most recently, the fire!"

"I know. But you must understand that you have been through a lot. We all have."

She nodded, eyes falling to the floor. "I will no longer stand in the way of your marriage to Patience. Not out of obligation but because I see now that you really do love her. I knew so at the ball but I allowed fear to cloud my vision. You are a truly wonderful, generous man of great character, always treating us with kindness, from carrying me home in the cold, to leaving your travels to make amends with Patience, and even saving Mr. Foster! Oh, Mr. Williams, however shall you forgive me?"

"I have already forgiven you, Miss Everleigh. You forget that I, too, am not spared of faults. I went against your better judgment without caring about the damage you faced. We all contributed to this moment, not simply yourself. Besides, I see you were only acting out of love for your sister."

"And I am afraid I went too far."

"As have I, for I am now second-guessing my desires if it brings you peace of mind."

"Oh!" Autumn protested. "Don't say such things! You and Patty have always dreamed of seeing the world! And even if you are injured along the way, you will heal. Besides, she has you, and you will keep her safe. After all, what is life without a little spice?"

Mr. Williams approached her and bent down, giving her a hug. "I am blessed with having a sister-in-law who is all but too kind."

"And I with a brother-in-law whom I shall get to tease."

They left the embrace and he turned to sit down across from Patience. He took her hands in his, and they locked eyes dreamily.

Autumn stood, the blanket falling from her shoulders as she took a few shaky steps and seated herself on the floor at Mrs. Glendale's feet. "I don't blame you if you don't want to talk with me."

"I have no preference," the woman whispered in a sob. "I sit in the sorrow that I have created for myself. I know you have apologised, and everything will work out as I wished it would, but I still think of Percy... especially now."

Autumn took one of Mrs. Glendale's hands and rubbed the surface as she stared up at her. "You loved him."

"Dearly."

"You know, there's a difference between remembering and forgetting to live, Mrs. Glendale."

"I do not wish to hear your judgement of my—"

"I have no negative thoughts toward you, for I have also lost and am reminded of my father's death every day." She pulled her father's ring off her finger, eyeing the distorted reflection of herself. "I have been living in the pain of the past and in fear for the future. I believe it's time I move on and remember my parents, without forgetting to live."

"What are you trying to tell me?"

"That I think it's time to let go, together. You have enjoyed wonderful days with Percy, with some not as great as others. You have laughed, cried, suffered, and even prospered. But you, too, can move on..."

"I only want to be the sister he deserved."

"And he would be so, so proud of you. So proud."

"No, not me, for I am a selfish woman who thinks only of herself."

"It doesn't have to be that way."

"How so?"

"Well, for one, I know of three loving children and a baby who would love to hear a good bedtime story now and then. Time goes by quickly, and before you know it, they will mature and be the ones taking care of you..." Autumn smiled at Patience as she raised her sore ankle. "And all you'll have left are the memories you made together."

"But how could they ever forgive me? After all I have done?"

"There is nothing to forgive. They are just waiting for you to come back to them."

Mrs. Glendale lowered her head against Autumn's chest, crying silent sobs. "I miss him so very much."

"I know you do," she rubbed the woman's hands, "I know."

Some whispering came from the door, and Marry-Elizabeth peeped around the corner.

Autumn and Mrs. Glendale eyed her.

"You may come in," Autumn said, inching back.

Mary-Elizabeth hesitated, then drew near. "Mama, are you crying?"

Mrs. Glendale nodded quickly, blinking away tears as she opened her arms part of the way. She stopped, as if scared to continue.

"It's okay," Autumn whispered.

Mrs. Glendale let out a slow breath as she extended her arms to Mary-Elizabeth, who obliged and returned the hug with glee. They held on to each other a long while, the mother gripping tightly and the daughter sympathising with her.

Autumn got up and hobbled to the door, her foot feeling a little better now as she gripped the doorframe.

Everyone was happy; Mrs. Glendale reunited with Mary-Elizabeth, Patience rubbing her hand in loving circles over Mr. Williams' cheek, and Autumn content watching them there.

"Excuse me," she said to a maid passing in the hall outside. "Would you direct me to Mr. Foster?" And Autumn left, heading upstairs and approaching one of the bedrooms as the doctor backed out, closing the door with a click.

"How is he?" she asked, pulling at the tips of her left sleeve and flashing her eyes between the man and the silent door.

The doctor smiled, revealing the wrinkles in his face as he answered calmly, "He's sore and has some minor burns, here and there, but he will be fine."

"May I?" she asked, pointing to the room with a shaky hand.

The doctor nodded, but Autumn had already turned the handle.

"Mr. Foster!" She rushed to his bedside, picking up his hands and squeezing them tight.

He lay on his back and smiled, lifting his heavy eyelids as if he believed that his happiness could not last forever. "Miss Everleigh, what are you doing here?"

"I had to see if you were all right. You are, aren't you?" She looked at his body, shuddering at the burns on his face.

"Quite. And now can write about what it's like to be in a fire."

Autumn touched her teeth together, thinking that his comment sounded quite sad indeed.

Much to her alarm, he started coughing hacking coughs and used a tired arm to cover his mouth.

"Here—" she let go of him to retrieve a cup of water from a table and held the brim of the glass to his mouth, putting her free hand on top of his. "Drink," she commanded, and he did.

After a few sips, he let his head turn away. "Miss Everleigh, I'm sorry that I—"

"Sh-sh-sh," she placed a finger against his lips, silencing him. "You have done nothing for which you should apologise." Autumn seated herself on the side of the bed and gingerly took his hand. She squinted at his features, as kind and innocent as they always had been, even despite his burns. Yet she saw him in a brighter light than she ever had before.

Mr. Foster smiled faintly and rubbed his thumb on top of her own.

Autumn closed her eyes. She had so much to say, but where to begin?

"Well, thank you." He gave a nod as he continued to circle his thumb over hers.

"For?"

"For being the only person in my life I could still see while being blind."

Autumn's heart melted at his words. At a loss as to what to say, she followed her impulse before she could change her mind. She leaned forward and kissed him on the cheek, letting her lips linger on his skin for several seconds, separating with a slight pop when she released them.

"I never expected I would ever, ever fall in love. Until I laid my eyes on you."

"And I never thought love could feel so wonderful until I heard a soul as soft as yours."

Autumn swooped down and sealed their mouths together, her fingers touching his soft hair. Neither withdrew until they needed to breathe again.

"I love you, my dear, dear Kendrick." She let out her breath, cheeks flourishing with colour.

"I love you, my darling Autumn."

They sat quietly happy for some time until Mr. Foster asked, "Is the window open?"

"Yes. Yes, it is. Shall I close it for you?"

"No, no. Would you describe to me what you see?" His curiosity made her want to hold him even tighter.

"Well," she smiled as her joy outshone the sun, and she fixed her eyes on Mr. Foster. "First, I see two dark eyes, full of kindness and curiosity, kindled with a sense of selflessness and a giving spirit. I see smooth, soft hair and a smile, a smile that says more than I have the words to describe. And beyond that is a mind, a mind so unique that everyone is blessed to be in its presence. And under that a heart, a heart I would die just to spend another minute with. I see the man of my dreams, my desired future husband, who I wish to forever spend my life with. And that," she added softly, "is all I see."

17

February 15, 1881

The A. & P. Express chugged out of Carlisle and off out into the world.

"Watch your step, my love," said Mr. Foster as he helped his wife take her seat on the train.

"Thank you." Autumn placed herself on the sky-blue love seat in their cabin.

"How grand!" Patience squealed from the couch across from them, hugging her spouse and pointing to the window displaying a various landscape of rivers and mountains. "How long 'til we get there?" She cupped her hands together against her chest, pursing her lips.

Mr. Williams checked his pocket watch. "About an hour or so."

Autumn gripped Mr. Foster's arm and smiled, her eyes taking in the surroundings of the carriage. The door opened. Two porters entered, carrying a stack of luggage, which would be needed for Mr. Williams' voyage around the globe. And to think that Autumn was going too! She couldn't imagine missing a chance to explore the world with her sister and create new memories together.

"Shall you write all about our travels?" Autumn asked her husband, resting her head atop his shoulder.

"Yes, my darling. I will have it titled: *A Man Travels the Globe with His Lovely Wife and the Happiness They Experience While Doing So.* Although this time I may write simply for our pleasure, without the need to publish."

"If you wish, I shall read your writings aloud to you every night under the stars before we sleep."

"Exquisite." He nuzzled his nose into her hair as she stroked his arm with one finger. My, how much she loved him!

"*Psst!*" Patience gave a harsh whisper, beckoning Autumn over with a wave of the hand.

"What?" She gave a long blink, pretending to be annoyed.

"Come, sit with me!"

Autumn rolled her eyes, smiling as she let go of her husband, then kissed him before standing.

"Mr. Williams, would you move to the other side?" asked Patience, forcing him up. He stepped into the aisle, gesturing to his vacant seat and smiling at Autumn.

"Thank you," she laughed, gripping the arms of the couch and seating herself beside her sister, purposely bumping against her arm.

"I wanted to show you something." Patience bent down with a groan and pulled their mother's old scrapbook from her bag, lifting it into her lap.

"Did you add something?"

"Yes. I ran out of space a few weeks ago, and so I replaced the pages with new ones." She pulled back the cover and flipped through the blank sheets.

"And whatever shall we fill them with next?"

"One can never tell, although I know each and every inclusion will display the coming joys we will share together."

"Then I suppose today is the start of a new page of memories."

Patience put a hand around her sister's arm, giving a small squeeze. "Today is the start of a lifetime of memories."

"Well!" Her face lit up and she leapt to her feet. "I believe that first page is waiting to be filled."

"What on earth do you mean?" Patience squinted, setting her fingers into her sister's extended palm, and rising.

Autumn said nothing, just took her by the hand. She led her sister through the door and into the next car.

The sisters exploded into a fit of giggles as they started to run, bolting through the crowded aisles.

"Come on!" Autumn laughed, leading the way and dodging in and out of bewildered passengers with Patience ducking behind as they hastened along.

They ran through car after car, adrenaline pulsing and hearts dancing as they reached the last car, empty save for a few crates and a firm staircase.

"Where are we now?" Patience asked, slowing to a stop and leaning over with a hand to her stomach. "My, that was fun!"

Air rushed from an opening in the roof, washing over the sisters and tangling their blonde and brown stands of hair together.

"Follow me," Autumn guided her up the steps at a steady pace.

"Are we going to the top of the train?"

"You shall have to wait and see!"

Autumn stopped halfway up, letting her sister pass her. "Go on."

Patience peeked her head up over the roof, mouth opening as she squinted from the sunlight. "Why!" she shouted above the wind and chugging of the train, "I can see a river!"

Autumn beamed, giving her a nudge to keep going. Patience shielded her eyes with one hand, scrunching up her nose as if bracing for impact and took a few more hesitant steps.

"One more!" Autumn encouraged.

"What if I fall?"

"I shall hold on to you, like so!" She slid her hand to Patience's waist, securing her with a firm grip.

Her sister took the last step, her body shaking as the train passed through the shadow of a sleek mountain.

"Be free," Autumn whispered.

Patience squeezed her eyes shut, took a deep breath and, in a quick movement, thrust both arms wide, tipping her head back as the sunlight poured over them both, exhilarating Autumn's soul.

"Isn't it wonderful?"

"Most extraordinary."

The train jerked, and Patience fell forward, fear flooding her eyes as she gripped Autumn's shoulders, sending them both off balance.

"Whoa!" The sisters laughed and hugged each other for stability.

They had come so far. They had argued, lost, fallen, and gained, and both had come out more mature and understanding in the end. And yet they were still the same sisters they had always been, two best friends sharing a fierce and enduring love from their youth, though now in brighter light.

Patience left the embrace, hair a mess, as she kept her hold on Autumn's shoulders, eyes locking in a blissful gaze.

"I love you, Autumn," she said, pressing her forehead against her sister's.

Autumn leaned into the hold, touching their noses together. "I love you, too, Patience."

They both opened their mouths and started to sing on the tips of a united whisper,

"Hum ditty, hum ditty, off in a daydream,
Won't you come and dance with me?
Hum ditty, hum ditty, off in a daydream,
Thank you for the dance with me..."

Acknowledgements

Let's be honest, you wouldn't be reading this book right now if not for the grace of God and the loving support of my incredibly *amazing* family, who stuck with me throughout this entire writing process, encouraging me to aim beyond my wildest dreams and achieve anything that I set my mind to, especially this project.

Mom, your selflessness will never cease to amaze me. It's quite evident that you constantly go above and beyond in your task to raise your children for the kingdom while educating and preparing us for the world. I cannot express how thankful I am for the increasing time we get to spend together, especially recently, as you pour into me through thoughtful conversations and experiences. You are the definition of an active mother, working hard and always going out of your way to bless others, and I honestly look up to you for it.

Dad, you continue to awe and inspire me 24/7 with your talents, skills, jokes, and social confidence, not to mention your ever-increasing knowledge and wisdom. It is an absolute blessing to have someone to connect with across all areas of life, from discussing world changes, diving into deep hypothetical conversations about our interests, to writing our books together and encouraging each other in the process.

If I have learned anything from you two, it's that I will bless the socks off my future kids, just as you have done for me and my siblings.

Of course, what would our family be without the greatest little sisters of all time—Kyree, Kenzie, and Kiki?

Kyree, I can't even remember life when you weren't my best friend and closest companion, and I still can't get over how powerful our friendship is to this day. We are so in sync with our thoughts and intentions as we truly connect on a level unlike any I have ever seen. I often feel as if we are both in our exciting little worlds together, where only we can understand each other to the full extent. Some of my favorite moments in life are the lengthy laughs and inside jokes that we share, the nerdy conversations we have, and the nighttime adventures gallivanting across the Disney theme parks together!

Kenzie and Kiki, you are further proof that family members make the greatest friends. You are truly the two greatest joys in my life, and I am beyond ecstatic to be your older brother.

Kenzie, your humor, wit, and laughs are life-giving, and I feel our relationship blossoms brighter every day. You are growing into such an intelligent young lady full of God's grace and goodness, and I am so beyond proud of you.

Kiki your profound energy and innocence are enough to make one cry, and I will forever adore the delightful presence you embody wherever you go. No matter the day, I can always count on you to dispel a sad scene with your bright enthusiasm and comedy.

I still can't believe how fast both of you are growing up, and I thank you both for being my greatest cheerleaders and official hosts of the "Unofficial Justice Fan Club"!

Allyce, my cat, literally sat beside me during this entire writing process, from concept to publication. Allyce, you kept me company through the early mornings, late evenings, and lonely writing days, and I honestly couldn't have written this book without you. Thanks, baby!

Moving on from family, I thank Abbie Emmons, the real reason this book ever made it beyond the outlining process in the first place. While I've never had the privilege of actually meeting you, that has not diminished the profound effect you have had on both this book and my writing life. When I first discovered you on YouTube, I had but a fragile idea of what a real story was, and now, thanks to your in-depth teachings, I am a more confident writer, with a finished book that I am proud of! If you ever read this, know that you have just caused another ripple effect in the world, changing my life and also the lives of those who are transformed by the message in this novel. God bless, and rock on!

Micaiah, I have been fortunate enough to have you as my best friend for almost a decade now, and one thing that hasn't changed is your kind and generous personality. I have never met a more supportive and encouraging person, and I am very confident that God is going to use your gifts for many extraordinary things. I am blessed to have had the opportunity of growing up and experiencing the major seasons of life with you, especially now as we continue to navigate the world as adults. Thank you for being there when I had no one else, allowing me to share everything under the sun with you. And thank you for continuing to shine your light on the world every single day! Love you, bro!

Mr. David and Mrs. Jeanette, the two greatest people of all time who, let's be honest, are practically family at this point—right?...maybe? I'm calling it now, you are both officially family! (Ignore what science says!) You inspired one of my favorite scenes in this book, which, if you know, you know.

Amy and Elisha: it's no secret that you continue to spread God's love wherever you go, never ceasing to deliver the gift of friendship and joy. I thank you both for cheering me on through this writing process, encouraging me with your honest support and contagious energy, and joining us on our many Orlando outings across the theme parks! You have an extremely bright future ahead, and I pray that the Lord will continue to use your talents to do incredible things!

Joshua, thank you for being the ultimate prankster and basically the little brother I never had. It's crazy how fast we became friends, and I must say that it's been a joy connecting and building a friendship over the past year! Talking with you is never short of some great laughs, jokes, and knowing you...pranks.

Mr. Joesph Yakovetic, I grew up without an extended family, so having the ability to talk and spend time with someone who actually cares means more than you will ever know. I thank you again for attending my graduation celebration and for being someone in my life I can look up to and connect with!

The McKellen and McNair family, for having such a massive impact on the most memorable seasons of my life. It has been a blast to reconnect again over the recent years, and I look forward to the next big "family" get-together!

Mrs. Connally and Mr. Matt, the aunt and uncle I never had! I want to thank you for being my lifelong champions and number-one supporters in all that I do! Visiting with your family is never without many laughs and good times!

Mr. Vaughn, having the opportunity to build our friendship means a lot. The fact that you treat me as an equal, given our age difference, is a true blessing. I will never forget the day I told you the plot of my story, as witnessing your reaction truly inspired me to continue with this book! Thank you again for coaching me to the finish line and welcoming me into your life as your friend!

"Uncle" Rob, hands down, you are one of my favorite people. I absolutely love your positive energy and people skills, and I legit laugh every time we hang out! One of these days, I am gonna surprise you at your house, maybe bring a cake too!

Mr. Mike Opidal, when I think of all the adults I am genuinely inspired by, you easily fall into the top of the top. I seriously admire your confidence and courage and find your closeness with God miraculous to watch. Thank you for welcoming me into the Giant community, being patient, and giving me the chance to learn from you and the team. I cannot wait to connect with you and your family in the near future! Until then, I keep you in my prayers!

The Sanchez family, for being energetic supporters in all that I do! All three of you are positively fantastic, and I am so fortunate to have people in my life who actually want to see me succeed! You're all the best!!

And lastly, my editors for *The Space Between the Seasons*, Becky, Margaux and Alison, who transformed my messy manuscript into the novel that you see before you today! Working with you was a pleasure, and I look forward to collaborating again soon!

From the very bottom of my heart, thank you, everyone.

About the Author

Thanks to his childhood spent making comics and stop-motion animation films, Justice Tilsher is now under the spell of creating three-dimensional characters and exploring the scientific formula behind society's greatest stories.

Aside from being a writer, Justice is also an unapologetic Christian, artist, entrepreneur, inspiring speaker, and jet skier.

Whenever he's not sharpening his skill set or volunteering in his local community, you can find him weekly at the Walt Disney World Resort in Florida with his family, or hacking the online business realm with his cat Allyce at his side.